Praise

"A true roller-coa[ster]... many twists and turns that even the most astute reader will be riveted to the stunning conclusion." – *Publishers Weekly, STARRED Review of The Broken*

Top Pick! 4 1/2 Stars! "Grips the reader from the first page. A definite must-read." – *RT Book Reviews on The Broken*

"When it comes to spine-tingling, nerve-jangling romantic suspense, Coriell delivers the literary goods...just the ticket for fans of Allison Brennan, Lisa Gardner, and Karen Rose." – *Booklist on The Buried*

2015 ITW Thriller Award Nominee - Best Paperback Original – *The Buried*

Romantic Times Reviewers' Choice Award Nominee – *The Buried*

4 1/2 Stars! "...inventive, well-crafted, detailed plot complete with a clever, diabolical villain..." – *RT Book Reviews on The Blind*

"Coriell delivers a winning, realistic blend of thriller and police procedural" – *Mystery Scene Magazine on The Blind*

Also by Shelley Coriell

The Broken (Apostles Series #1)
The Buried (Apostles Series #2)
The Blind (Apostles Series #3)

Information on these books and others can be found at
www.shelleycoriell.com

Rough Day

Detective Lottie King
Mystery Short Stories, Vol. 1

Shelley Coriell

Winter Pear
Press

This is a work of fiction. Names, characters, places, and incidents are products of the author's imagination or are used fictitiously. Any resemblance to actual people, living or dead, or organizations, events, or locales is entirely coincidental.

Published by Winter Pear Press
Tempe, AZ

www.winterpearpress.com

Editing by Linda Style

Cover Design by Clarissa Yeo

ISBN 978-1-944439-01-9

To Paula Slone

Table of Contents

Rough Day

A Detective Lottie King Mystery

Chapter One

Forty years ago Lottie King buried a Smith and Wesson 9mm under a peach tree sapling in her backyard. Not a typical place to hide a murder weapon, but if the police came looking, she figured they wouldn't be too interested in the freshly turned earth.

Today hundreds of peaches hung ripe and heavy on the old tree, enough to keep Lottie's seven grandkids and half of Colorado Springs in peach pie for a week. She took this as a sign that forty years ago, she'd done good.

"Hey, Grandma." Emmie perched in the crook of the tree, her fingers curled around a rosy globe. "How's this one?"

Lottie eyed the seven-year-old with catawampus corkscrews atop her head. "Perfect."

Emmie plucked the peach and dropped it into the basket balanced on Lottie's hip.

The phone at Lottie's waist buzzed. Caller ID showed Scott Traynor.

Emmie gazed at her through the branches, peach leaves sending shadows across her cheeks. "Do you have to answer that?"

Lottie wasn't on call, so technically she didn't have to, and frankly, she didn't want to. Today was Saturday, her first day off since that nasty business with the serial killer known as the Broadcaster Butcher two months ago, and she planned on spending every moment with the grands—baking peach pie, tossing the pigskin, and kicking ass at Mario Kart. With a jab of her finger, she sent her partner to voicemail. "Nope. I'm taking the day off. I need me some serious R&R."

"Mom's worried about your heart." Emmie grabbed another peach and pulled. "She says you need to retire." Tree leaves bounced in absurd laughter.

"My ol' ticker's in tip-top shape, Emmie-Bug." Lottie thumped her chest. Her heart was the reason she kept working. If she retired, she'd have a gaping hole in the middle of her chest. She loved her job: catching killers.

"Can we make ice cream in a bag, too?" Emmie asked. "Bella's Girl Power troop made it last week. I snuck some. It was epic."

"Epic? I'm thinking we might need to investigate."

Emmie giggled and plopped the peach in Lottie's basket. That giggle—a grand's laughter—was one of the best sounds in the world.

The damn metal mosquito buzzed at Lottie's waist. Traynor. Again.

"This better be important," she said with a low grumble as she took the call.

"Just got called out to a double at Old North End." An uncustomary softness accompanied Traynor's voice this morning, not a hint of the razor-sharp edge honed by too many years of seeing too many dead bodies. "One of the victims is Ruthie Kells."

The basket slipped from Lottie's hip, but she lunged,

saving Emmie's two perfect peaches before they crashed to the hard-packed earth.

"I'm the lead, and Caruso is backing me up," Traynor continued. "I thought you'd want to know." He cleared his throat. "And Sarge, I'm sorry."

***

Lottie parked her car, an arthritic Jeep Cherokee minted in the last millennium, in front of a sunny yellow Victorian with a wrap-around porch. It was a beautiful old home on a quiet, wooded cul-de-sac, but for the past twenty years this place had housed folks, mostly women, who'd seen a whole lotta ugly. Ruthie Kells was the founder, chief fundraiser, and head gardener of Ruthie's Place, a shelter for victims of domestic violence. She was also one of Lottie's oldest and dearest friends.

They met more than forty years ago in a GED class at one of the local churches. Both teenagers with babies on their hips, they had plenty of miles on their thrift store shoes. After getting her GED, Ruthie hit the road running. She sprinted through college and law school and logged in some impressive miles at the district attorney's office before opening Ruthie's Place. Lottie took a more winding route, suffered a bit of road rash, and added two more babies, but in the end, both she and her long-time friend ended up with careers battling Big Bads.

Of course Lottie was too close to Ruthie to work the case, but she wanted to make sure Traynor and his team knew she had skin in the game.

On the back porch she found Traynor slipping into a

pair of paper booties. "Coroner's with the bodies, and the photog just finished."

"Big Bad?"

Traynor ran a hand through his straw-colored hair. "Nothing yet."

She snapped on booties and a pair of latex gloves. Thirty years ago when she first joined homicide, she remembered wanting something heavier and sturdier than paper and plastic to shield her from the evil that awaited inside. Damn, had she been stupid. These days she invited evil, breathing the barbarity and brutality into her lungs and bloodstream, and used it to fuel the fight for good.

She followed Traynor across the back porch to the first victim: the door. Even in fair weather, Ruthie kept all doors and windows buttoned up. Her old friend was determined to keep out users, abusers, and shit-for-brains losers. In the twenty years Ruthie had been running the shelter, she never had any violence. Lottie stepped around the pile of wooden splinters that had once been a door.

In Ruthie's kitchen Lottie paused at the body sprawled on the floor. Young Hispanic woman. Double tap to the head. "Our shooter knew her," Lottie said.

She squatted, her old knees creaking. The victim wore worn jeans and a ratty T-shirt. Probably in her twenties. Average weight, height, and looks, but there was nothing average about the black and purple swelling around her right eye, lacerations on her bare feet, and bracelet of bruises around her right wrist.

"Got an ID?" Lottie asked.

"Not yet. No purse. No suitcase. Empty pockets except for a handful of change. We're assuming she was a guest seeking shelter from an abusive situation."

Lottie rose and stepped around the two-foot pool of blood haloed around the young woman's head. "Ya think?"

Women seeking shelter at Ruthie's Place often arrived with the clothes on their backs and baggage they didn't carry in their hands. Ruthie would open her door and offer a hot cup of coffee and a new shot at life. Lottie cupped a gloved hand around one of the coffee mugs on the kitchen table. Still warm. She pictured the terrified young woman finding comfort in that cup and in Ruthie's calm but steely presence.

Lottie searched for that calm and steel and let them settle into her bones. "Second victim?" Ruthie.

Traynor jutted his chin toward the doorway at the far end of the kitchen. "In the dining room. Looks like she was trying to get away."

"Bullshit." Lottie jammed a finger at the young woman splayed on the floor. "Ruthie fought for battered women. There's no way she'd run and leave behind one of her girls in need."

Traynor studied his right shoe. "Of course, Sarge."

A long wooden table that could and had seated a dozen guests at one time sat in the center of the room. An old pie safe of white pine snuggled against one wall, and along another was a tiny yellow and blue plastic picnic table with its customary stack of coloring books and bucket of crayons.

She spotted the slippers first, old and comfy, the blue

faded to gray and fleece flattened. No flashy heels for Ruthie. Next Lottie zeroed in on the blood. Dizziness rocked her.

"Single GSW to the chest," Traynor said.

A streak of blood snaked across the length of the room, and bloody handprints clutched the back of one of the dining chairs. Ruthie had fought to the end.

A hard, knobby lump lodged in Lottie's throat. "Witnesses?"

"Neighbor to the east heard three shots. Thought it was a car backfiring. When he went into his backyard a few minutes later to eat breakfast, he spotted the shattered door and called nine-one-one."

"Any other guests in the house?"

"We found a single guest room in use, so it looks like just one."

A smile threatened Lottie's lips. Ruthie always said she'd die happy if she saved *just one*. Over the years, one turned into one hundred, and Ruthie was probably closing in on one thousand. But in the end, Ruthie had died anything but happy. The fist jammed down Lottie's throat and sucker punched her gut. There were so many hellish ways to die: trapped without air, consumed by fire, tortured by a human who practiced the inhumane.

But the worst hell was personal. Ruthie had died knowing she failed to save *this one*.

Lottie widened her stance to steady herself. She closed her eyes, breathing in the fresh smells of coffee and—

The skin on the back of her neck pebbled. Her eyes flew open. Traynor was hunched over Ruthie's body, and the CSI photog was packing gear into a large roller box. For a full minute she didn't move except for the rippled flesh inching down her spine.

"Can you, um, give me a minute of privacy?" Lottie asked her partner.

Traynor nodded and snapped his fingers. "Guys, take five."

After their footsteps faded, Lottie sat on the bench of the kiddy picnic table, the plastic groaning under her weight. "It's safe," she said. "You can come out now."

Silence. Not even a whisper of breath.

"I'm a friend of Ruthie's," Lottie continued. "I brought the plate of turtle brownies over last weekend."

At last a shuffle sounded in the pie safe, followed by a scrape. The cupboard door creaked open. A bare foot peeked out, followed by a leg covered in a faded pair of sweat pants, then a shoulder, finally a head. A woman, probably in her mid-thirties but who looked a decade older, crawled out of the pie safe. No wounds. No blood spatter. But terror had etched deep grooves across her forehead and at the corners of her eyes.

Lottie, still perched on the child's table, held out her hand. It was an unthreatening hand—soft, cocoa-colored, and wrinkled, like the double Dutch chocolate cookies she baked last month for Traynor's birthday. "My name's Lottie."

The woman cast a skittish glance to the men standing mouths agape in the doorway as she sat. "I...I'm Doreen." She wrapped her arms around her body as if trying to fold into herself and disappear.

"Doreen, I need to know what happened this morning." But first Lottie needed to give this woman control, something that had most likely been missing much of her life. "When you're ready, I want you to describe in your own words what happened. Take as much time as you need. No detail is too small. Everything is important. I'm going to keep you safe. Do you understand that, Doreen? You're safe."

The woman rocked to the rhythm of Lottie's words. *You're safe. You're safe. You're safe.*

Some clod in the doorway let out a huff that Lottie silenced with the look she usually reserved for lowlife, maggot-infested, slime-sucking child molesters.

"The new girl got here about five this morning," Doreen finally said. "She was pretty roughed up and scared. We went through a full pot of coffee before she stopped shaking. Sometime during the second pot, a guy started busting up the back door. Ruthie told us to run out the front. The new girl didn't move. I tried to pull her away, but she went to him. *To* him! Stupid. Why did she do something so stupid?"

Because she thought she could stop him. She thought that if she loved him hard enough and begged him long enough, she could put an end to the chaos and crazy that was their life. Bullshit.

"What happened next, Doreen?" Lottie prompted.

"The guy took out a gun and... and shot the new girl. She screamed and screamed. I didn't think I could make it to the front door with my bum leg, so I crawled into the cabinet, shut the door, and hid."

"Did you get a good look at him?"

"I saw nothing."

"But you heard?"

"Everything." Doreen rocked faster as if trying to shake off the horror. "He fired another shot, and the new girl, she called herself Jane, she stopped screaming. The silence, oh God, it was worse than the screaming. "*Rock, rock, rock.* "Even the little girl got quiet."

Every muscle in Lottie's body tensed. "Little girl?"

"Jane had a daughter. Sophia, I think was her name."

The men hovering in the doorway froze.

"She was five, maybe six," Doreen went on. "Poor little thing was exhausted. A few minutes after they got here, Sophia fell asleep on the couch in the living room."

Lottie, Traynor at her heels, rushed into the adjoining living room and skidded to a stop in front of the couch, empty but for a worn afghan and throw pillow. "What happened to the girl? Where the hell's the girl?"

Doreen stood at the doorway. "After the man with the gun shot Jane, he demanded to know where Sophia was. Ruthie..." Doreen's chin trembled. "Ruthie said the child wasn't here, that this was a place for adults only, but we could all hear the little girl crying in the living room. He ran past the pie safe, and Ruthie must have followed. That's when I heard the next shot and felt the floor shake." She turned from those old, faded slippers. "I figured he grabbed the kid and left because I didn't hear any more shots or crying, just running feet."

Traynor motioned to the men in the kitchen. "Caruso, check every cupboard, vent, and closet where a child could hide." Because best-case scenario was Sophia hid and, like Doreen, was too frightened to come out. "Daniels, get a neighborhood roadblock set. Brimmer, check with dispatch and see if we had any calls from a woman fitting our Jane Doe's description. I'll get on the Amber Alert and call in the Feds to get a CARD team out here."

Her partner turned to her. "And you?"

The first few hours in a missing child case were crucial. A handful of minutes could be the difference between hugging that sweet baby or grasping air. "I'm going to help you track down that baby-stealing son of a bitch."

Chapter Two

After finishing his call to the FBI, Traynor jammed both hands through his hair, which now resembled an untidy haystack. "My guys scoured this place, Sarge. How the hell'd you know that woman was hiding in the pie safe?"

Lottie had smelled Doreen's fear and heard the woman's rapid-fire heartbeat because Lottie had lived it, something none of the men in this house could ever understand. But she'd also smelled the coffee. She pointed to the kitchen table. "Two cups of coffee. Ruthie only drank tea, so I figured she must have two guests in the house."

"Thank God you were here."

"Thank me after we find the girl." And nab Ruthie's killer. Damn, she wanted a piece of this maggot.

Since their Jane Doe had sought refuge in a domestic violence shelter, the kidnapper was most likely a domestic partner, possibly the girl's father. They could be looking at a custody battle turned into full-scale war. The problem was, they had no last name or a solid physical description.

According to Doreen, the little girl had long, dark brown hair and wore an oversize, pink T-shirt. "And pink sandals," Doreen added. "With sparkly jewels in the center. I remember because Jane said Sophia loved them and insisted on wearing them to bed."

The other issue: They had no description of the abductor or his vehicle. All they had right now was a ticking clock, and with each minute, their search area grew. Time to strike fast and close.

Next door Lottie and Traynor found Ruthie's neighbor still in his pajamas and sitting before a plate of congealed eggs. "We've never had anything like this happen in the neighborhood. Things have always been so peaceful at Ruthie's house. This is..."

"Wrong," Lottie said. "And it could get worse. We believe the shooter took a small child, a five- or six-year-old girl. Did you see her?"

"I saw no one."

"Do you have any security cameras?"

He shook his head.

Neither did Ruthie. Her friend always wanted to install cameras, but she never had enough money at the end of the month. "How about any unfamiliar vehicles?"

Another head shake.

"What about sounds? Did you hear a child's voice or cries?"

He poked his rubbery eggs. "You know, now that I think about it, I do remember hearing a kid crying, but it came from the greenbelt that runs along Monument Creek. I figured maybe a kid fell off his bike. Today we're having a community bike parade."

＊＊

It was a beautiful mid-August morning. Perfect day for peddling in the park. Or picking peaches and making ice cream in a bag. Lottie took out her phone and texted Emmie: STILL @ WORK. WHY DON'T U INVESTIGATE THAT ICE CREAM IN A BAG?

Emmie texted back: ON THE CASE. :-) :-)

Not one but two smiley faces. Duly noted.

Now time to catch a killer.

Lottie and Traynor topped a slight incline that dropped to the greenbelt along Monument Creek when she spotted something glinting half way down the hill. A sharp jolt raced down her legs, and she took off, her shoes pounding dead leaves and twiggy ivy. She skidded to a stop before a pink, sparkly sandal. Her stomach dropped. "Oh, sweet baby!"

Once in the greenbelt, she and Traynor threaded their way through one, two, and three-wheeled cycles decked out in balloons and streamers, desperately searching for a girl with one pink shoe. A couple on a bright yellow tandem swerved around her, and a little boy on a red moto-cross bike tooted his horn. "Out of the way, lady!"

At the water station, a woman with a floppy sunhat sat in front of a bucket of ice.

Lottie flashed her shield. "We're looking for a man and a little girl, not on bikes. They probably walked through here about an hour ago? She had long, brown hair and a pink T-shirt."

"Sure, I remember the girl," the woman said. "She was not a happy camper, upset that she lost a shoe. The man refused to go back for it."

"What did he look like?"

"Youngish, I guess, maybe in his twenties, big guy. I think he was wearing a baseball cap."

"Which way did they go?"

"I'm not sure. A big group of bicyclists stopped, and I had to hand out water bottles."

Lottie and Traynor hurried down the bike path. The nearest parking lot would be their best bet. Someone abducting a child wouldn't do it on foot unless he was stupid, but the truth was, most criminals had a degree or two in stupidity.

They reached the parking lot when a voice called out, "Wait!"

Behind them the woman with the floppy sunhat darted between balloons and bikes. "Ice cream," she said on a huff when she reached them. "I remember the guy saying he'd buy the girl ice cream if she'd just shut up."

"Did he say where?" Traynor asked.

"No, but she stopped crying and said she wanted vanilla swirl with rainbow sprinkles."

Back in the cul-de-sac, they hopped in Traynor's car. Lottie pulled out her phone. "Ice cream," she said into it. Less than ten seconds later a map popped up with seven places that sold ice cream within a two-mile radius.

"You've done this before?" Traynor said as they barreled out of the neighborhood.

"Yep."

"These places sell ice cream at nine in the morning?"

"Yep." Grandmas knew shit like this.

Somewhere this little girl had a grandma. Did she know her granddaughter was missing? Her daughter was dead? Lottie leaned forward, urging the car to go faster.

At a nearby convenience store with a soft serve machine, the clerk reported no ice cream sales. When they reached the fast food restaurant next door, the manager pointed to the drive-thru window. "Talk to Julie. With the bike parade, she's had cars lined up all morning."

"Yeah, I sold ice cream this morning to a guy with a kid," Julie said.

"Little girl?"

"Yeah. Lots of pink. She got a vanilla swirl with rainbow sprinkles. He got a supersize Coke."

"Did he pay by credit card?" *Please, please.*

"Cash."

Damn. "What did he look like?"

"Dark hair I think. Or maybe he was wearing a dark cap. Kind of a big guy."

"What about the vehicle?"

"It was a truck. I'm sure of it, because the little girl sat in the passenger seat and wasn't buckled. After he got their order, he spun out of here crazy-fast. I remember thinking the girl was going to get killed."

Lottie was dealing with supersize stupid. This guy was a child abductor and murderer. "Do you remember the color, make, or model?"

"Older truck, a small one. It was dark, black, I think, and no tailgate."

"You got that?" Lottie asked Traynor.

Traynor held up his phone. "Already updating Amber."

***

When she was a baby homicide detective, Lottie learned all about Locard's Principle: You enter a place, you leave something behind. You leave, you take something with you. Most of the time it was stuff you couldn't see with the naked eye. At a crime scene, the CSI boys called it trace evidence. She called it essence of stupidity.

Ruthie's killer most likely left a piece of himself at Ruthie's Place, and Lottie wanted it something fierce. Techs had found a shitload of prints in the kitchen and living room, and right now Frank Porter from the FBI's Child Abduction Rapid Deployment team was running them through IAFIS, the FBI's mother of a fingerprint database.

Lottie stood at Agent Porter's left shoulder. "What's taking so long?" Lottie tapped her foot on the tile floor of the war room that had been set up at the station to house the ever-growing number of bodies searching for little Sophia. "I thought these computers were supposed to be faster than lightning. My oldest grandson could have conquered five bosses by now."

Traynor poked his head through the doorway. "Just got the report from dispatch and nine-one-one. No domestic violence calls last night involving a woman with Jane's description to us or to neighboring jurisdictions. No hospitals within a hundred mile radius with record of our Jane. Still no sign of the black truck."

In police work, they walked around sticking giant pitchforks here and there. Eventually, they'd hit something and get a squeal.

Agent Porter clicked the mouse. A mug shot popped

on the screen.

"Hellooooo, mama," Lottie said on a rush of air. "That's our Jane, Sophia's mother. Why'd she pop?"

"Her prints were on the red coffee mug on the kitchen table."

Lottie leaned over Agent Porter's shoulder and squinted at the screen. Jane Doe was Amanda Olivarez, a twenty-five-year-old female with an address in a low-rent area off South Nevada. "What put her on the books?"

"A few counts of disorderly conduct, possession, and"—the FBI agent mouthed an obscenity—"child endangerment."

Lottie had no issue with swear words and belted out some of her finest.

Agent Porter switched to another screen. "Looks like last January the mother, Amanda Olivarez, went to a skeezy motel room to shoot up with a boyfriend and left the kid in the car. It was twenty degrees that night. Child protective services swooped in and turned Sophia over to the grandparents until Amanda got herself cleaned up. No problems since then. According to Amanda's case-worker, she had been on the straight and narrow. Full-time job, parenting classes, regular NA meetings."

Sometimes it took losing what mattered most to get folks to make a few lifestyle changes. The thought of someone taking away that precious baby forced Amanda Olivarez to get her crap together, which probably meant dumping some garbage along the way.

"Give me the guy," Lottie said. "There's a stinkin' guy somewhere in her past."

Agent Porter made a clicking sound with his tongue.

"No mention of any abusive relationships. No talk of drug dealers. No word on the little girl's father."

"No worries," Lottie said. Because they finally had something. A name.

Chapter Three

Amanda Olivarez may have died broke and broken, but she'd been born into money.

"Please come this way, Sergeant King and Agent Porter." A housekeeper in a boxy navy dress led them across a foyer made of fancy stone laid out in a giant medallion pattern. "Mr. and Mrs. Olivarez will see you now."

In a sunny atrium, a middle-aged woman sat on a bone-colored sofa, a man in smart golf attire standing behind her, his hand on her shoulder as if to keep them both steady.

The woman's fingers clenched tightly, her fingertips morphing into over-ripe cherries. "It's Amanda, isn't it?"

Lottie loved her job, except at pisser moments like this. "Your daughter was involved in an incident at a domestic violence shelter."

The woman choked out a groan, the kind that seeded deep in the gut.

Lottie cleared her throat. This kind of stuff should get easier with each passing decade. Yeah, right. And she should still fit into size six jeans. "A gunman entered the shelter and shot both your daughter and the shelter's director. Your daughter died on the scene."

That groan tunneled its way through the woman's innards and spilled over the twisted gash of her lips. "It's our fault. We said Amanda wasn't welcome here until she got herself off the drugs. We cut her off financially and even threatened to take away So—" The woman's face turned the bleached bone color of the sofa. "Sophia! Did something happen to Sophia?"

"We believe she's still alive."

"Believe?" Mr. Olivarez asked with a roar.

Here was pisser-moment number two. "The gunman took Sophia. She's missing."

"Where is he? Who is he?" Mr. Olivarez demanded.

"We're hoping you can tell us." Agent Porter took over the questioning. "Where is your granddaughter's father?"

"He died before Sophia was born. OD'd on heroin."

"Did Amanda have any men in her life? Any prone to violence or that she was afraid of?"

"No, not recently," Mr. Olivarez said. "She was getting her life together. No more abusive men. No more drunks and druggies."

Mrs. Olivarez twisted her hands, her cherry fingertips turning into blueberries. "There is that young man named Tommy that Sophia mentioned."

"That guy who babysits?" Mr. Olivarez asked.

Mrs. Olivarez nodded. "Amanda blamed us for CPS taking away Sophia, and she doesn't let us spend time with Sophia anymore, not even to babysit. When I called last week, Amanda was in the shower, so Sophia and I got to chat. My granddaughter sounded wonderful and said Amanda was doing great and they were going to church where they met a friend named Tommy who watches her while her mom goes to work or NA meetings. Sophia said Tommy was a good guy and didn't smoke pipes or use needles." Mrs. Olivarez gave her head a sad shake. "Sophia's a smart kid, wise beyond her years."

A kid smarter than her druggie mom. This was one screwed-up world.

"Did Sophia mention a last name?" Agent Porter continued.

Mrs. Olivarez shook her head. "Just Tommy."

"We'll need Amanda's address, phone number, church information, along with—"

"My apologies." The Olivarez's housekeeper hurried into the room clutching a cordless phone. "But you have a call, Mrs. Olivarez. He said it's urgent."

"Take a name and number, and I'll—"

"He said it's about Sophia. His name is Tommy."

With a strangled cry, the grandmother dove for the phone, but Lottie, even in her four-inch espadrilles, was faster. Lottie placed her finger over the receiver and said softly, "You have to keep calm. For Sophia."

"You need to keep him on the phone as long as you can." Agent Porter fished out his cell. "We're going to try and get a trace on the call."

"Listen for background noises and voices," Lottie said. "And get Sophia on the phone."

"We need proof of life," Agent Porter added. "Ask him to send a photo or video or e-mail or leave a note in Sophia's handwriting in a public place. The more connections we can make, the better chance we have of saving your granddaughter."

The grandparents nodded, and Lottie held out the phone. Mrs. Olivarez reached for the phone, then froze. She swallowed twice then motioned to her husband. *Poor thing, too choked up to talk.* Lottie set her hand on the woman's shoulder.

Mr. Olivarez took the phone and pushed the speaker button. "Yes, Tommy. What can I do for you?"

"Oh, about a half-million things." His soft chuckle slammed into Lottie's chest like a wrecking ball. This was the voice of Ruthie's killer.

"Is Sophia with you? Is she safe?"

"Yes and yes, and she will be as long as you do exactly what I say. I want half-a-million dollars."

"Put Sophia on the phone."

"She's watching cartoons."

"I need to talk to her. I need proof she's alive."

"You need to do what I tell you." Tommy's words came out sharp and panicky.

"We'll do exactly what you want, but first the proof." Mr. Olivarez, a successful businessman, was negotiating the most important deal of his life. Tommy had already killed. Twice.

At last there was a sigh on the other end of the line then footsteps. Lottie closed her eyes, better to focus on background noises. Soft shuffling. A squeak. Tommy wore tennis shoes.

"It's your grandpa," Tommy said. "Tell him what kind of ice cream we had for breakfast."

"Vanilla swirl." The voice was small and so, so far

away.

"With?" Tommy said.

"Rainbow sprinkles."

Mrs. Olivarez rested her forehead on her knotted hands and nodded.

"So here's the deal, Gramps," Tommy continued. "I want the money tonight."

Lottie and Agent Porter shook their heads.

"Banks can't get me that kind of money on a Saturday," Mr. Olivarez said. "We need more time."

"You don't have time. Amanda assured me you have money coming out your ass, so I suggest a bit of personal excavation. Now listen good because I'm only going to say this once. Be at the county fair in Calhan at nine tonight. Bring the cash. I'll call right before the drop to let you know the exact location. If you bring cops or involve anyone else, little Sophia will not live to eat another bowl of vanilla ice cream. With or without rainbow sprinkles."

"Send me a picture of So—"

The phone went dead.

Lottie turned a hopeful gaze on Agent Porter whose grim lips spoke without moving. No-go on the trace.

Mrs. Olivarez grabbed Lottie's hand. "What now?"

"We will continue to use every resource we have to track down your granddaughter," Lottie said. "The FBI's CARD team will continue to sift through forensics, and my men are all over the streets. Saving Sophia's life is our main objective."

After they found the child, Lottie would personally scoop up the pile of shit that killed Ruthie.

***

Lottie: BAD GUY STILL ON THE LOOSE. CAN'T LEAVE.

Wasn't the first time someone in her family got this text message from her, and it wouldn't be the last.

Emmie: OK. :-(

Lottie stared at Mr. Frowny Face. This was the kind of job that interfered with peach picking, and, blessing of all blessings, her family understood, even the little ones like Emmie. But that didn't mean they liked it. Nor did she, but she had a killer to catch.

Members of the multi-jurisdiction taskforce were ramped up and running, ready to find the little girl who loved vanilla ice cream with rainbow sprinkles. The FBI was identifying and locating child sex offenders in the area while uniforms were beating on doors of local businesses looking for security footage that might show a black truck with no tailgate. At this point, getting a pop on that ride was their best chance of saving Sophia.

Lottie and Traynor had spent the afternoon searching Amanda Olivarez's one-bedroom apartment furnished with nineties cast offs. No signs of Tommy. The neighbors on either side didn't remember seeing Amanda or Sophia with a man, but the nosy neighbor in the corner apartment said she noticed a piece of mail in Amanda's mailbox from the Grace for All Church.

The smells of grilled meat and woody smoke greeted Lottie and Traynor as they arrived at a BBQ fundraiser for the youth group at Amanda's new church. The kids were out of burgers and brats, so Lottie bought a pair of grilled black bean burgers—her middle daughter who was always harping about her less-than-healthy eating habits would approve—and handed one to Traynor, and they tracked down the pastor at one of the picnic tables.

"Sure, I remember Amanda and her daughter," the pastor said. "Amanda was a member of one of our single mothers support groups, but I don't ever remember seeing her with a man."

Ditto for the twenty-two other church members they interviewed.

"It's like we're chasing a ghost," Traynor said as he tossed their burger wrappers in the trash.

"We're chasing a man who doesn't want to be remembered."

"You think he had kidnapping for ransom planned all along?"

Agent Porter and his CARD team knew about kidnappings, but she knew about dead bodies. She'd been around enough of them to know they spoke to those who listened. She pictured Amanda's black eye and bruises circling her wrist.

"I'm thinking Tommy Buttmunch had money on his mind from the beginning, but not necessarily ransom," she said. "He found out Amanda's family was loaded and befriended her and Sophia, probably with a meet-up in the church parking lot. When he finally put the squeeze on Amanda, pressing her to get at the fam's money, he discovered she'd been cut off by her parents. He wouldn't take no for an answer, and he roughed her up, but this time, she had her kid on the line."

Lottie pictured Amanda's bare feet and pocket of change. "Determined to take care of her kid, Amanda managed to slip away from Tommy, grab Sophia, and run. No time for shoes or a purse, but she did grab a handful of change from a bowl, the one on her kitchen counter. Amanda ran off into the night. Unfortunately, she had nowhere to go. She wouldn't go back to her old druggie friends and thought she couldn't go to her parents. She found a payphone and called someone who'd been in her situation, probably one of the women in her single mothers support group. The woman sent Amanda straight to Ruthie's Place, and that's how our shooter found out about the shelter. He must have caught up with her after she escaped and tailed her to the shelter."

Lottie fell into a deep silence and waited, but that's all Amanda Olivarez's dead body had to say.

***

It was a great weekend for a county fair. Clear skies. Just enough wind to spread the smells of Indian fry bread and roasted corn but not enough to kick up dust at the rodeo arena and dirt track.

As promised, Mr. Olivarez had come up with five-hundred-thousand dollars, and he was ready to deliver.

Lottie pulled her ancient Jeep next to a white van. Agent Porter was already inside, working the controls at one of the screens.

"You ready, Sergeant King?" Agent Porter asked when she climbed into the van which was full of gizmos and gadgets designed to track down missing babies.

Lottie locked gazes with Mrs. Olivarez, who sat on a bench in the back of the van as one of the FBI agents outfitted her with a wire. "A grandma's gotta do what a grandma's gotta do," Lottie said as she sat and accepted a wire of her own.

At nine on the dot, Mrs. Olivarez's phone rang. Restricted number. Agent Porter nodded to Lottie, who picked up the phone.

"Hello," Lottie said. "This is Maria Olivarez." Not true, but the catch in her voice was genuine. She couldn't help but think of little Emmie, her granddaughter.

"Are you at the fairgrounds?" Tommy asked.

"Yes. Is Sophia here?"

"She's someplace safe."

"I need to talk to her."

"No can do."

"So, she's not with you right now?" As Lottie spoke, techies were hard at work getting a fix on the call.

"She's safe."

"Give me proof. I need to know my sweet baby's alive."

"Shut! Up!" A soft rustle sounded. The guy was running his hands through his hair. Maybe wiping sweat from his forehead. Deep breath. "Now listen. You will pick up a bag from the welcome table. Put the money in the bag. Then go to the food court and leave the bag at the base of the garbage bin near the frozen lemonade stand at 10:08. Not before. Not after."

"Why 10:08?" *Hang on sweet baby, we're getting close.*

"Because I said so."

"And my Sophia?"

"Once I get the money, you'll get your granddaughter."

"Alive and unharmed. Promise me she'll be alive and unharmed."

"I said—"

"Damn it, promise me!"

"Keep your granny-panties on, lady. Fine. I promise."

"Good." Lottie forced her heart to slow. "But nothing happens until I talk to Sophia. Put her on the phone."

"You're hardly in a position to make demands."

"I'm begging you, please. Please put my little Sophia on the phone." Her voice cracked, and it wasn't part of the acting job. "I need to hear my grandbaby's voice."

Grumble and growl. A door opened. Shuffle and rustle. No other footsteps or voices. Tommy was alone.

"Grandma?" The single word warbled. "Is that really you?"

This was not a child of her blood, but that voice cut straight to Lottie's heart. "Yes, it's me, sweet baby, and we're going to get you home real soon." Lottie didn't bother to disguise her voice. Little Sophia was probably confused and afraid, but her grandmother, the real one who was sitting next to Lottie with her back ramrod stiff and ready to fight, said she was also smart. "Now here's what I need you to do..."

***

Lottie pushed the stroller through the fair entrance and up to the welcome tent, keeping a good thirty feet between her and Mr. and Mrs. Olivarez. She wasn't worried about a spotter. Tommy was working alone. Nonetheless, she bent over the blanketed bundle in the stroller, a doll one of the beat boys kept in his cruiser to give to scared little girls, and made cooing sounds. Then she checked her watch.

9:37.

She grabbed one of the large canvas totes the fair was giving out as a freebie today. On it was a teen-age boy with a dimpled smile and mop of wavy black hair.

"Jacob Fleet?" Traynor asked as he stopped next to her and picked up a Jacob Fleet bag of his own. Her partner wore jeans, a cowboy hat, and a little dust, as if he'd just left one of the rough stock events.

"A shiny new pop star for the bubblegum crowd," Lottie said. "My twelve-year-old granddaughter, Bella, loves the kid. Looks like she isn't the only Jacob Fleet fan."

A swarm of fairgoers buzzed through the fairgrounds, most toting Jacob Fleet bags.

"Holy crap," Traynor said under his breath, and Lottie agreed. Keeping a spot on a Jacob Fleet bag full of a half-million bucks just got a hell of a lot more difficult.

9:58.

Lottie bought a funnel cake topped with gelatinous strawberries and strolled down the dusty aisle to a group of picnic tables five yards from the garbage bin where the Olivarezes would make the drop. Traynor sat at the table behind her.

"You're stewing," Lottie said.

"Why 10:08? Do you think it's a number of personal significance?"

Lottie bit into the ropy cake, the bite landing with a greasy thud in the pit of her stomach. "Tactical." She aimed her fork at the fair schedule printed on a table tent. "Jacob Fleet's concert ends at ten, and everyone and their Great Aunt Rosie is sweet on Fleet." Lottie stabbed her fork into her cake. "Now eat your deep-fried cupcake and look like you're having a good time."

10:02.

It started as a trickle. A few teen-age girls walking from the amphitheater and down the food court aisle, many wearing heart-shaped *Sweet on Fleet* glasses. Lottie took three more bites of grease and sugar, each barely making it down her throat.

10:05.

Then came the flood. A crush of bodies descended upon the midway. Squealing tween and teen girls, their parents, and some folks in cowboy hats, because the last rough stock event also ended at ten. Their boy was only half stupid.

10:07.

Lottie kept her gaze drilled on Mr. and Mrs. Olivarez, who elbowed their way through the mass of human flesh, the ransom demand sandwiched between them.

10:08.

The grandparents dropped the bag. Walked away.

Lottie stood and grabbed the stroller handle, deserting the cake. He was here. He was close. And he was hers.

She strolled through the crowd keeping her eye on the trashcan. Just an old grandma, albeit one with kick-ass shoes, taking care of a sleeping grandbaby while the rest of the family rode coasters and spun in teacups. A pair of girls, their heads bent and giggling, crashed into the stroller. She steadied the fake baby, the girls, and herself.

She reached the trash bin.

10:09.

The funnel cake in her gut twisted back on itself. The bag was gone.

She spun. Dust rose, coating her sweaty limbs, scratching her wide eyes.

Where the hell was he?

She swatted away the dust and grasped only air. The baby-stealing son of a bitch was gone.

Chapter Four

10:19.

"What now?" Mrs. Olivarez said, her voice shrieky. "We're supposed to get Sophia *now.*"

Lottie unclenched a hand from the stroller handle and turned down the volume on her headset. "Be patient," she said into the mic tucked behind her ear. "He'll get word to us." Because this is what was important. Getting the lead on the child. Saving *just one more.*

Back and forth, Lottie strolled, looking to all like she was soothing a fussy baby while really searching for Ruthie's killer.

10:32.

A text came through on the Olivarez phone: CHECK THE FOURTH ROOM IN THE FUNSTER SHACK :-)

"Funster Shack?" Agent Porter's voice boomed in her ear. "What the hell?"

"The fun house near the roller coaster," Lottie said. "My grands loved it when I brought them to the fair last year."

She ditched the doll and took off through the midway, hurdling a schnauzer and carving a path through a group of Jacob Fleet fans.

At a building with rounded corners and a checker-board paint job, a pimple-faced ticket-taker waved her back. "I'm sorry, ma'am, this attraction is only for guests under one-hundred pounds."

"I am. These pants just make me look fat." She pushed through the turnstile.

A sea of black flooded the first room of the Funster Shack. Using her hands, she groped along the walls through a twisting corridor. With each turn, the ceiling sloped lower, forcing her to her hands and knees. She squeezed through an oversized mouse hole, her hips scraping the sides, and landed in a room with a zig-zag-patterned floor. She stood. The floor boards shifted. She righted herself.

"This is not fun," Agent Porter said from behind her.

In the next room Lottie hopped on a large spinning disk. On the side near the door, she prepared to jump when a plastic clown with a blow-up sledgehammer bopped her on the head.

"I'm going to be sick." Agent Porter was green.

"Spot up on the door."

This time when the spinning floor reached the door, she pushed aside the clown and jumped.

Three rooms. One more to go. "We're coming, Sophia," she called out.

After two twists, the corridor opened into a room of mirrors and a million kids. No, more like a dozen multi-plied by the mirrors. Distorted faces were everywhere.

"Sophia!"

No one answered.

A dark haired girl stood in the corner sticking her

tongue out at herself. Lottie ran to her, but smacked into a mirror. She groped along the wall until she reached the girl. Too tall. Wrong eye color.

"Everyone out!" Agent Porter clapped his hands.

As the room emptied, Lottie eyed the mirrors, going from left to right, up and down. At last she spotted a small piece of paper, one of them little yellow sticky notes, in the lower corner of a wavy mirror. She reached for it but hit cold, hard glass.

"Find the yellow sticky note," Lottie said with a growl. Or maybe that was the funnel cake twisting and grinding in her stomach. "The chump's buying himself time and wasting ours."

Agent Porter scrambled alongside her and called out, "Got it!" The seasoned agent's hands shook. "Says the girl's in a culvert two miles up the road."

But was she alive?

***

Within ten minutes, Lottie was hopping out of Agent Traynor's van and hauling ass through scrubby brush to a long, wide drainage ditch. In front of her, flashlights bobbed through the gritty haze of dark and dust.

To her right, Agent Porter called out, "Found her!"

Be alive. Please, please let that baby be alive.

Lottie skidded to a halt in front of a large concrete pipe.

Agent Porter was on his knees before a pink bundle. Everything stilled. The soft wind. The swirling dust. The bundle.

"Oh, sweet baby," Lottie said with a strangled cry.

The mound of pink let out a muffled cry.

Lottie raised both hands to the heavens where a soul like Ruthie surely rested.

Just one more! *You hear that, Ruthie. I got you just one more!*

Sophia, her arms and legs bound by rope and duct tape over her mouth, frantically blinked at Lottie.

Agent Porter hopped up and patted Lottie's shoulder. "I think she wants you."

Lottie tore her gaze from the heavens and dropped to her knees. Now that Ruthie got hers, it was time for Lottie's. "I'm Sergeant King, the one you spoke to on the phone." She tucked the edge of her fingernail under the duct tape covering the girl's mouth. "We need to get this off quickly. You know that, right?"

Blink.

Lottie yanked.

"He's driving a blue car, kind of old," the girl blurted out, "but I couldn't see the license plate."

Lottie crumpled the tape in her fist. The plan had been for Sophia to get a solid ID on the guy's ride.

"But," the smile on Sophia's face reached her eyes, "I got the license plate number off the black truck. 525-JMF. That'll help. Right?"

Lottie wanted to scoop Sophia into her arms, hold her, and tell her over and over how brave and smart she was. Instead, Lottie rested a hand on the child's head. "Unlimited vanilla swirl ice cream with rainbow sprinkles for a year, young lady." She called over to Traynor, "Got a license plate number on the black truck."

"I'll get out an APB," Traynor said.

Which wouldn't do them any good as the truck was probably parked in some hidey-hole because this Big Bad was only half stupid. He must have seen or heard the Amber Alert, which had folks looking for a black truck with a missing tailgate.

"I'll get a name on the truck's registration," she said, because with a name came stuff like cell phone accounts, and with cell phone accounts came phones, and with phones came GPS tracking systems.

Smart phones were arch enemies of stupid criminals.

So were smart little girls.

***

Less than an hour later, they got a spot on the cell phone for Robert Prykowski, aka Tommy Buttmunch, aka Ruthie's killer. A signal pinged off a cell tower in Washington County. He was heading northeast, and Lottie and Traynor took off, following the happy pings. At two in the morning, the techs reported the smart phone and stupid criminal stopped moving.

"He's east of Fort Morgan off the I-76," Lottie said as she studied the cell phone data. "There are a few truck stops, motels, and a handful of residences."

Time to put some juice into her lime-green espadrilles. After canvassing truck stops, they hit one of the motels.

"We're looking for a man in a blue car," Lottie told the motel manager. "Would have come through here within the past two hours. Dark brown hair, five-ten, about two-hundred pounds. He's most likely wearing blue jeans, a black T-shirt, and dark gray Nike tennis shoes with a light gray stripe." Double scoop of rainbow sprinkles for Sophia because she also got a good physical description.

"Yep. He's here. Room fourteen."

A wash of warm, tingly sparks rushed across Lottie's skin. This was why she worked months without a day off. This was why she could walk away from peach pie and ice cream in a bag. Like Ruthie, she always wanted *just one more*. Just one more criminal off the streets. Just one more killer behind bars. Just one more win for justice.

The sparks reached Lottie's heart and set it on fire. *This one's for you, Ruthie.*

Lottie took off toward the east wing.

Traynor grabbed her arm.

She tried to pull away, but he clamped tighter.

"I'm the lead on this, Lottie," Traynor said. "I'm taking you off."

Her *junior* partner had spent too much time today in the sun. That freckled nose of his looked awfully red. "Listen, Hayseed, Ruthie was one of my best friends. She was the one who babysat my girls when I needed help. She was the one who loaned me money to make the down payment on my house. *She* was the one I was going to cruise the Caribbean with when we both retired." Lottie jabbed her hand at the motel. "That sorry excuse for a human being in room fourteen made her last moments on earth a living hell." Because Ruthie hadn't been able to save *just one more*.

"Exactly, Lottie. Ruthie was a *friend*."

"Who needs me!"

"Not like this." Traynor grabbed both of her shoulders.

A frosty breath rushed through her lungs, and she realized she was shaking. Her shoulders. Her hands. Her legs. Her heart slammed against her ribcage. Sweat trickled down the center of her back. Because she was about to face her best friend's killer.

"You're welcome to wait near the manager's office or in the car." Traynor let go but squared up in front of her. "You're not going in."

Because right now, right here, she was a friend. Not a cop. Traynor was right. She had no business busting into that room. She had too much skin in the game. She steadied her quaking body. "I trained you well," she said.

"Agreed." Traynor waved down the trio of sheriff's cruisers pulling into the parking lot, and within minutes they were setting up for the collar.

Lottie paced from the vending machines along the front of the motel to the pool and hot tub at the back. Her arches ached, and the linen straps of her espadrilles cut into her ankles.

Traynor, decked out in SWAT gear, approached the door. "Colorado Springs Police!" *Bang. Bang. Bang.* "Open up!"

Silence.

"We can do this the hard way or easy way." Her partner took the key the manager gave him and unlocked the door. Still no sound. He cracked the door. "Last chance. Come out walking on your own, or we're coming in."

Silence.

Traynor and one of the locals burst through the open door, service revolvers extended. They ducked inside. Her heart slowed. One agonizing beat. Two. Three.

"Not here!" Traynor called out.

Damn that foul, stinkin' pile of shit. She ran to the room. The bulging Jacob Fleet bag sat on the bed, and clothes were on the floor: jeans, T-shirt, socks, underwear.

"The money's still here," Traynor said. "He can't be far."

Lottie couldn't take her eyes off that underwear. Naked. Their guy was naked. Where the hell would a naked man go? Her feet twitched, and she darted out of the room.

A lone man sat in the bubbling hot tub, his eyes closed against the swirls of steam.

"Soaking off a rough day?" Lottie asked.

The man jerked upright. "Yeah." He reached for a towel on the edge of the hot tub.

She unholstered her Glock and aimed it at Ruthie's killer. "Too bad. It's about to get rougher."

Chapter Five

Lottie kicked off her shoes and left them in the front entryway along with her bag. She'd pick up tomorrow. It was after three in the morning, and she needed sleep.

A mound on the sofa in the living room stretched and asked, "Rough day?"

Lottie found the energy to smile. It was Tiarra, her youngest daughter who lived down the block. Your life was a good one when your kids chose to buy houses just down the street. She sat on the edge of the sofa and patted her daughter's leg. "Let's see. Today I attended a bike parade and a few places that sold ice cream. Then I went to a church BBQ and the county fair. Finally, I ended the day at one of them hot tubs."

Tiarra sat, pulling off the nubby throw. "And a fun time was had by all, I'm sure."

"The ending wasn't too shabby."

Tiarra unfolded her legs and wrapped her arms around Lottie. "I'm sorry about Ruthie."

Lottie nodded but not hard enough to let the tears welling in her eyes spill on to her cheeks.

With one more hug, Tiarra slipped on her sandals. "I'll go ahead and take Emmie home and let you get to bed."

"Emmie's here?"

"She insisted on staying. Said you two had big plans."

Peach pie and ice cream in a bag. Important stuff in a seven-year-old's world. A smile snuck past the tired. Hers, too.

"You head on home, Tee," Lottie said. "Emmie can stay here tonight, and tomorrow, we'll get to those plans." She kissed Tiarra's forehead and watched her daughter walk to her house where Will and the triplets were fast asleep.

The light over the kitchen sink glowed. Emmie sat on a wooden stool at the kitchen counter snoring softly, her arms and head pillowed on a bag of flour. The basket at her elbow held six perfect peaches.

Lottie was about to lift Emmie and take her to the spare room when she thought of her old friend who was always ready for *just one more*. One more life to save. One more bit of good to put back into the world.

Lottie flicked on the kitchen light. At the sink, she squirted a giant dollop of soap onto her palm and cranked the faucet. Water spurted and tinkled into the stainless steel sink.

Emmie opened one eye. "You're home."

"Yep."

She opened the other eye. "You catch the bad guy?"

"Yep." Lottie dried her hands on a worn tea towel and pulled a large mixing bowl from the cupboard.

"You going to make peach pie?"

"Yep."

"And ice cream in a bag?"

"Yep." Lottie slid the mixing bowl to Emmie, then reached for the basket of peaches. "It's gonna be epic."

Emmie giggled.

Ice Cream in a Bag

Cool and fun-to-make, this easy dessert is perfect for kids of all ages!

Yield: Serves 2; Prep time: 10 minutes; Total time: 10 minutes

Ingredients
1 cup half-and-half
2 tablespoons sugar
1/2 teaspoon vanilla extract
1/2 cup rock salt
About 8 cups of ice cubes
1 pint-size zipper plastic bag
1 gallon-size zipper plastic bag
Your favorite mix-ins: fresh fruit, crushed peanut butter cups or candy bars, cereal, etc.

Directions
1. Combine the half-and-half, sugar, and vanilla extract in pint-size bag. Seal.
2. Place the ice, salt, and pint-size bag in gallon-size bag. Seal. Shake the bags until the half-and-half mixture hardens, about five to ten minutes.
3. Take the small bag out of the large one. Add mix-ins.
4. Eat straight from bag.

Author's Note: I first made this fun dessert with my three daughters, then pre-school age, during one of Arizona's notoriously hot summers. Forced indoors by 110 degree temps but needing to do something active, we prepared bags for each of us, turned on some upbeat music, and danced. Ten minutes later, ice cream! This also works well with large groups. My Girl Scouts loved it. My favorite mix-in: chocolate toffee bits. Detective Lottie King would definitely add chopped peaches. Enjoy!

From the creative kitchen of award-winning author
Shelley Coriell
www.shelleycoriell.com

Locked Room

A Detective Lottie King Mystery

Chapter One

Something dug into the soft space between Detective Lottie King's shoulder blades. Cold. Hard. Cylindrical. *Holy shit*! A gun.

She inched her hand to her hip, stretched her fingers, and grasped flannel. Flannel? Where the hell was her Glock?

She cracked an eye. The room was dark. She was stretched out on something soft. Smelled of dryer sheets. A bed? Her eye adjusted to the darkness. *Her* bed. The clock on her nightstand read eleven. In the morning. On a Sunday. Why that was the butt-crack of dawn. She turned to give whoever was poking her tired old body a look that would blister the fuzz off a peach.

Kass, her middle daughter, stood above her with a deadly glare of her own. "You're late."

Lottie pulled the covers over her head. "For what?"

The sheet snapped back. Kass aimed a stick at her. "For the Girl Power meeting you're supposed to be leading right now."

Lottie squinted at the stick. Orange. Metal. Glittery globe in the center. A handheld lightning rod. "Son of a bitch!" She threw off the sheet. Winced. Her shoulder injury, a stab wound from that dust up with the Broadcaster Butcher, was still giving her fits. "I got a lead last night on that low-life suckwad who killed the twin coeds. We snagged his ass at eight this morning."

But she had to get moving. For Bella's Girl Power troop. She swung her legs over the bed and heaved herself up. Check that. Halfway up.

A hand landed on her shoulder, pushing her back onto the bed. Kass's eyes softened, and she tucked the lightning rod in the back pocket of her jeans. "It's okay, Ma, we can reschedule for next week. The girls will understand."

"Nope. I made a commitment." Lottie patted Kass's hand then pushed it aside. "Got to follow through. These girls need to understand and respect shit like that."

Lottie threw on a T-shirt and pair of jeans. Technically, she squeezed into a pair of jeans. She seriously needed to lay off the late night taco runs, but with her schedule, she didn't have time to make those kale and mango smoothies Kass was always nagging her to drink.

Teeth brushed. Hair pulled back in a not-so-tidy bun. Lottie joined her daughter in the kitchen. "Are you going to drive or me?"

"Where's your snack?" Kass asked.

"Snack?"

"You signed up to bring the snack."

"Double damn and a truckload of shit!" Lottie had planned to pick up the meeting snack yesterday on her way home from work. No worries. A Girl Power guide was always prepared. She rummaged through the freezer and pulled out a bulging bag.

Kass's jaw dropped. "You're bringing *cookies*?"

"Watch your language, young lady." Lottie caressed the plastic zipper bag. "These are brown butter salted caramel snickerdoodles."

"They're full of processed sugar and fat. The girls need healthy snacks. If you want to bring something sweet, why don't you bring stuff for yogurt parfaits?"

"Don't got no yogurt. Don't got no parfait." If she did, Lottie probably wouldn't have the tractor trailer tire around her middle, but now was not the time to contemplate her nutritional choices. "I got a Girl Power meeting to lead." Lottie tucked the cookies in her purse.

Kass looked at the ceiling and sighed. "It's supposed to be a two-part snack."

Lottie reached back into the freezer and pulled out a bag of lime-tequila chicken wings. Before her daughter could give her the stink eye, Lottie said, "It's not like I'm giving 'em shots of tequila, so put a lid on it."

As they pulled out of the driveway Kass asked, "What lightning bolt are you working on?"

"Son of a bitch! I left my notes and supplies at work." She had planned to help the girls earn their Public Speaking Bolt. Every girl needed to know how to find her voice and use it, a lesson Lottie hadn't learned until life knocked her on her ass a few times.

"You want me to drive to the station?" Kass asked.

Lottie worked homicide for Colorado Springs PD— the best job in the world—and her office was a good twenty minutes away. "The meeting will be half over by the time we get back." She grabbed the Girl Power Guidebook from her purse. She was a cop, fast on her feet and used to dealing with the unexpected. Thumbing through the pages, she saw so much good stuff in here to help build strong young women. Hiking Bolt? Too much walking. Book Artist Bolt? The only thing she could draw was a chalk outline of a dead body. Nutrition Bolt? *Snort.* She reached the last page: Create Your Own Bolt. Lottie thumped the page. "Perfect."

"What are you going to do?" Kass pulled into her driveway, her home just down the street from Lottie's place.

"What I do best." Lottie was out the door before the car came to a stop.

"Hey, Ma," Kass called after her. "Remember, you're not at work. No swearing."

Yep, she should probably give up bad words, too, a not-so-good habit she'd picked up while chasing down all those Big Bads.

Inside the house, six-year-old Amber was sitting at the dining table. "Hey, Grandma."

Lottie went to place a kiss on her head but jumped back. "Holy shi...bang!" Lottie jabbed a finger at the beady-eyed creature atop Amber's head. "What the hee-haw is that?"

"Choco. My new pet."

Lottie scratched at a corkscrew sticking out from her temple. "It's a rat."

"Yep. I want a dog, but Mom and Dad think I need to prove I'm responsible with a pet that's lower mainte-nance." Amber patted the creature sitting on her head.

Lottie turned to her daughter. "You got my grand-baby a rat for a *pet*?"

"They're small furry rodents that are intelligent and particularly good with young children. Look it up on the Internet. They're much better pets than hamsters."

"They're brilliant," Amber added. "Okay, Choco, show Grandma what you can do. Jump, Choco, jump!" The rat flew from the child's head to the kitchen counter and with bony, crooked, ratty paws picked up a chunk of hardboiled egg. "Cool, huh? Want to pet him?" Amber picked up the rat and shoved the pointy nose and twitching whiskers into Lottie's face.

Lottie jumped back. "Maybe later." Or never. Right now she had impressionable twelve-year-old minds to mold.

She found the girls in the Girl Power troop on the back porch. Three sat on the steps talking, three tossed a Frisbee, and two were swinging from the tire swing hanging from the mulberry tree. No texting. No playing games on phones. No posting photos on social media. Not a single cell phone in sight thanks to Girl Power Meeting Rule Number Three: Power down. Dang, she loved this kind of stuff. Kids couldn't be kids when tethered to all them electronic devices.

Lottie lifted the bags of chicken wings and cookies. "Time to get the bi-monthly meeting of Girl Power Troop #806 started. Bridget, take the cookies and arrange them on a platter. Aitana, get out a baking pan. Brooke Lynn, read the instructions and get these wings a cookin'."

With the snack set up, Lottie led the girls through the kitchen, grabbing a piece of chalk from the message board hanging near the phone. Once in the garage, the girls placed their sit-upons in a circle in the empty parking bay. Chalk in hand, Lottie squatted and drew.

"Sa-weet," Natalee said.

"Ma!" Kass said from the doorway. "What are you doing?"

"Drawing an outline of a dead body." Julia stated the obvious.

Lottie waved the back of her hand at her daughter. "Go inside and make sure that rat hasn't bitten my grandbaby and given her the Bubonic Plague." Lottie tossed the chalk to the side and dusted her hands. "This meeting has officially begun."

"What are we going to do?" Markayla asked from the edge of her sit-upon.

Lottie picked up the orange lightning rod. "Investigate a murder."

"A murder," the girls murmured in unison.

"Yep. Happened 'bout thirty years ago. One of the trickiest cases of my career." Lottie aimed the lightning rod at the chalk outline. "Ladies, meet your murder vic, Chickie Brown."

***

'bout Thirty Years Ago

Lottie picked her way through a maze of rotting tires, over a crumbling brick wall, and under the crime-scene tape. "Evening, Sarge. Where do you want me?"

Sergeant Hank Gorman popped the end of a matchstick between his lips, working it from one side of his mouth to the other and back. After the second roundtrip, he said, "That'll be up to you, *detective.*"

"Excuse me, sir?" Lottie asked.

He stepped aside, giving her full view of a single car garage with sagging roof and frayed coat of blue paint. "I'm giving you the lead on this one."

A warm, tingly spark shot up Lottie's legs. She'd been working homicide for a year and had always played second fiddle. 'Course that's where she belonged. She was the greenhorn and had spent the past year fine tuning her instrument, practicing, working hard, and learning from those who had more years in the band. Now it was her turn. The spark shot to her fingers, and she pulled a spiral notebook from her big bag. "My victim?"

"Benjamin Brown, known on the streets as Chickie Brown. He was found this afternoon with a gunshot wound to the head. Nineteen years old. Officially unemployed, but he's been associated with Izzy Torino's meth machine."

"Meth?" Lottie scrubbed a hand along her chin. "Man, that's some nasty stuff. Eats your brain. Causes memory loss and paranoia. Puts holes in your skin and rots your teeth. Bad, bad stuff. All drugs are bad. They'll ruin your life."

"Agreed," Sergeant Gorman said. "Word on the street is Chickie Brown joined Izzy's gang at age thirteen, first as a rat-runner then as a full-fledged distributor. Brown has quite the history and a rap sheet to prove it. Burglary, assault, possession of an illegal firearm. He got out of jail three months ago after serving time for distribution."

"You think his death is related to Izzy Torino?"

"I'm more interested in what you think." The matchstick made a final pass, and the sergeant motioned to the uniformed officer standing at the side door to the garage. "Watson was the initial responder. He can bring you up to speed. Good luck, Detective King, and may justice be served."

Justice. That's what catching killers was all about. Justice for all, even for a guy like Chickie Brown. He may have walked the wrong side of the law in life, but the law would be on his side in death.

"Evening, Detective King." Watson greeted her with a nod. "Body's inside."

"Who found him?"

"His mom." Watson pointed to a thin woman standing on the back porch of a small but tidy house, a sweater wrapped around her trembling shoulders and an oxygen tank strapped to her side. "After Chickie got out of jail, he moved into his mom's garage. When he didn't show for dinner this evening, she went looking for him. Saw him through the window. She tried to get inside, but the door was locked. She used a spare key, but a security chain held the door in place."

Lottie toed the shattered glass in the doorway. "She busted in?"

"The mom was too weak, so she went next door, and the neighbor and her son used a shovel to break the glass. The neighbor reached inside and unfastened the chain. Brown was not breathing and cold to the touch. The mom called nine-one-one." The officer dug into his pants pocket and pulled out a piece of paper. "Got a witness list for you. Contact info on the mom and neighbors on both sides." He handed her a disposable camera. "I also got pictures of people walking or driving by who seemed interested in the scene."

She fisted her hand and tapped Watson's shoulder. "Excellent work, officer." When you were in charge, it was important to acknowledge good work of those on your team.

Now to walk through the door to death. She stepped into the garage, black droppings crunching under her heels. Mice? Cockroaches? Probably both. She slipped both hands into her trouser pockets because the number one rule when investigating a crime scene was *Don't touch anything.*

She swept her gaze wide, getting a general assessment. Ten by fifteen feet. Single bed with a sour-smelling mattress. Sink with brown rings. Toilet with browner rings. A mini refrigerator held together with a bungee cord. There was also a fancy-pants stereo system and shiny new TV/VCR. Something with a scaly tail skittered along the wall and ducked under a pile of old gardening tools. She slid her camera from her bag and snapped photos from each corner of the room. *Snap. Snap. Snap. Snap.*

Now to narrow her focus. Chickie Brown lay on his back on the bed. He wore low-riding jeans, a striped ruby shirt, and a pair of chunky gold chain necklaces. *Snap.* GSW to the center of the forehead. *Zoom. Snap.* A 9mm Jennings, typical of the junkers found on the streets, lay in the middle of the room. *Snap.* Could be the murder weapon, or maybe the kid was protecting himself. Ballistics would confirm. The front wall was a wooden garage door on a giant rusted spring. *Snap.* A long u-bolt sat in a rusted lock covered with a lacy curtain of spider webs.

Her finger paused over the shutter button.

"Hey, Watson." Something soft but prickly, like a hundred wriggling spider legs, crawled down the back of her neck. "Did the neighbor or mom report seeing anyone else in the room?"

"No."

"You've been here the whole time?"

"Yep. Haven't budged."

The spiders moved down her spine. "You saw no one in this room?"

"No."

She checked out the ceiling. Sheetrock construction. No attic door. She walked the circumference of the room, tapping her heel every two feet. No hollow sounds indicating a door to a basement or cellar. Also, no holes in the drywall.

Lottie pulled out her Glock. "Cover for me," she whispered to Officer Watson.

He took out his service revolver. Extended his arms.

She listened. For breathing. A heartbeat. She poked under the bed. Slid open the tattered shower curtain. Opened the cupboard below the sink.

At last she holstered her sidearm.

"What were you looking for?" Officer Watson asked.

"The killer."

Watson's hand, still clutching his piece, bobbed. "He's still here?"

"The side door was chained. Garage door is bolted. Both from the inside. There are no windows, vents, or doggie doors." Lottie spun in a slow circle, taking one last look at the room. "There's no evidence of a bullet passing through the walls, ceiling, or garage door. Nor is there any way someone could have shot Chickie Brown and escaped."

Watson opened his mouth but didn't speak. The air grew still. Even the rodents stopped skittering.

"So how did Chickie Brown end up with a bullet in his head?"

Lottie stared at the victim's lifeless hands.

"You think he committed suicide?" Watson asked.

***

Present Day

"That's it?" Aitana sunk back on her sit-upon, the whoosh of air a breathy rush of disappointment. "Chickie Brown killed himself?"

Bella picked at the seam of her jeans. "Uh, Grandma, this is kind of lame."

"At least we have a great snack." Natalee hopped to her feet. "Those chicken wings smell great. I'll go check."

"Wait!" Markayla held up both hands and motioned Natalee to sit. "There has to be more. Sergeant King said this was one of the trickiest cases of her career. It's been too easy." The girl turned to Lottie, a glint lighting her eyes. "There's something else going on."

Lottie fisted her hand and popped Markayla on the shoulder. "Excellent work, officer."

Chapter Two

'bout Thirty Years Ago

Lottie eyeballed the handgun found near Chickie Brown's body. Would they find his prints on the gun? Was this really a suicide?

While the tech from CSI lifted prints off the door, Lottie, who'd been trained in latent, reached into her bag and pulled out a small kit with a squirrel-hair brush, print powder, lifting tape, stiff paper, and her library card.

***

Present Day

"You're joking, right?" Brooke Lynn asked, her eyebrows askew. "We need a *library card* to collect fingerprints."

"Library cards are incredible things," Lottie told the Girl Power crew. "With a library card you girls can score knowledge, adventure, even a little love between the pages of a book. Everyone needs a library card, including homicide detectives." Lottie dug a print kit from her purse along with a few pairs of latex gloves and her library card. "Now Julia, pick up the squirrel brush and open the silver powder. Note that we're using aluminum, a nice light powder. If we are trying to pickup a print off a light surface, like a wall, we'll use..."

"...dark powder," Kate said. "Probably carbon based."

"Correct." Man, these girls were geniuses. "Julia, you need to dab the ends of the brush into the powder. Just a bit. Too much and you'll fill the ridges. Too little, and there won't be enough contrast. Now touch and swirl. *Swirl. Swirl.* Lift." Julia lifted the brush, revealing a perfect fingerprint on the lightning rod. "Now your turn, Brooke Lynn. Place the tape an inch from the print, and using the *library card*, smooth the tape over the print. That little ol' card is what gives us complete adhesion. No air bubbles. Then pull and secure the print to the glossy fingerprint card. Label the card with the date and your name."

Perfect execution. "Okay, next pair of girls. Your turn."

***

'bout Thirty Years Ago

Lottie found four perfect fingerprints on the grip of Chickie Brown's gun. "Get these down to the lab ASAP," she told the evidence tech. Once there a pair of eagle-eyes would compare to Brown's fingerprints already on file.

A compact man with a bald head and bushy black eyebrows appeared in the doorway. The Great Dondini. A homicide detective was only as good as her team, and

Dr. Don Kovach was one of the best. Folks called him a magician because he was good at pulling case-solving clues out of thin air, or in his case, dead and decaying bodies.

It took a special kind of human being to be a coroner. Someone who didn't mind a body fluid or two, who could stomach maggots and the smell of raw hamburger left in a lunchbox for a month, and who could keep all those acronyms straight.

After Dr. Kovach finished his preliminary exam, Lottie asked. "CMM?" Just three letters, but they had a big ol' bearing on any death investigation. Cause, mechanism, and manner.

"Cause of death is perforating GSW to the right frontal lobe. Mechanism is exsanguination. He bled out."

"Time of death?"

"The body loses about one point five degrees per hour after death, so given the ambient temp, I'd say the victim died between ten and noon today."

Lottie stared at the gun at the side of Brown's bed. Now for than final M. Manner. Was she looking at homicide or suicide or even an accident? A good homicide detective needed to throw a wide net in the early stages of her fishing expedition. "Suicide?"

"Stippling at the entry point indicates shot fired from close range. Less than a foot. I'll be able to confirm when I get him back to the lab and open him up to see the trajectory through the cranium."

None of the above meant *pending*, which meant the clock was still ticking. Most homicide cases got solved within the first forty-eight hours. Time to open a few more doors.

She opened the cupboard under the sink where she found a half-empty box of cereal. Next, the refrigerator: expired milk, moldy olives, a Styrofoam container from Taco Tilly's. She snapped open the lid, letting loose a wave of spicy, tomato-y, chicken-y goodness. Tortilla chicken soup. She checked the receipt taped to the lid. Purchased this morning. Was this cup of chicken soup supposed to be Chickie Brown's last meal? If so, why didn't he partake? Was his suicide unplanned? Had something or someone rocked his world?

Next, she opened the nightstand drawer. You could tell a lot about a soul by what he kept in a nightstand. Address book, pen, key ring, city map, a few pieces of dried cereal, and a folded piece of notebook paper, one word written across the front: *Momma*

She unfolded the paper.

I'm sorry for all the trouble I caused, especially to you. I love you and will see you on the other side. Chickie

"You called this one, Detective King," Watson said. "Looks like Chickie Brown committed suicide."

***

Lottie heard Rowena Brown well before she saw her. A raspy wheezing followed by short puffs of air came from inside the small but tidy single-story house. Chickie's mother sat in a plush brown recliner in the living room, an old shoebox in her lap and a tissue clutched in her hand.

Lottie stepped over a plastic tube tethering Rowena Brown to a large tank of oxygen. "I'm detective Lottie King, Mrs. Brown, and I need to ask you a few questions about your son." *Was he suicidal?* Because right now everything in this investigation pointed to suicide.

Chickie's mother dabbed at her eyes with a shredded tissue. "Benjamin was such a good boy."

If you didn't count the fact that he dealt drugs and had a thing for breaking and entering. Lottie shuffled her feet.

"I know what you've heard, Detective King, and I'll admit, Benjamin made some bad choices, but he wasn't a bad boy. He was kind and sweet and would do anything for his momma."

"That's nice to hear, ma'am. I—"

"Every year for my birthday he gave me a hand-made card." She dipped her bony, thin-skinned hand into the shoebox on her lap and pulled out a card with an origami bird on the front. "Nineteen years old and still made his momma cards. Now, that's a good boy." Next she pulled out a piece of construction paper covered in lopsided hearts. "This was the first one he made me. He was in preschool. This is the one..."

Lottie was on the clock, but she was also in the living room of a woman who would soon be burying a dead child. As Mrs. Brown handed her card after card, Lottie acknowledged the colorful art and sweet way he signed his name, *Benjamin* with a heart over the letter *j*. Surprising stuff from a kid like Chickie Brown. But then again, not surprising. Not everyone was pure bad. Just like not everyone was pure good.

When she reached the last card, Mrs. Brown clasped the box to her chest. "During the past three months Benjamin has been at my side, taking me to all of my chemo appointments, handling all of the medical stuff, and even bringing me soup. My boy was good to his momma."

"I'm sure he was." Good people made mistakes. They sold drugs. They stole things. They hurt others and themselves. Lottie cleared her throat. "Mrs. Brown, when did you last see Chickie alive?"

"Benjamin!" Mrs. Brown dropped the box, cards spilling across her lap. "My son's God-given name is Benjamin."

"Of course, ma'am."

"I saw him two days ago, on Friday morning. He took me to a doctor appointment."

"What was his state of mind?"

"He was attentive, but quiet. Definitely more quiet than usual."

"Any idea why?"

"He said he had work stuff on his mind."

"I thought Benjamin was unemployed."

"Oh, no. He's been working at a call center getting insurance leads. They made him manager of his calling pod last month. Got a nice little bonus and bought me this fancy recliner. Like I said, Benjamin was turning his life around."

Lottie lifted the paper evidence box at her side. "Have you seen this before?"

Mrs. Brown nodded. "The gun belongs to Benjamin. At night he kept it on his nightstand."

"His nightstand?"

"This isn't the safest of neighborhoods, and he used to hang out with some rough individuals. He wanted something close at hand so he could protect us."

Now on to the hard stuff. "Did Benjamin ever talk of killing himself or wanting to die?"

"Suicide? Are you suggesting my son committed suicide?"

"We found this." Lottie showed Mrs. Brown another evidence bag, this one containing the note she found in Chickie's nightstand drawer. "Does it look like his handwriting?"

The mother's fingers trembled just above the note, as if she couldn't bear to bring herself to touch such horrific words. "Yes, but he'd never kill himself. He—" A hacking cough cut off the words.

"I know this isn't easy, Mrs. Brown, but we need to put your son to rest, and in order to do that, I need to ask some tough questions." At the grieving woman's nod, Lottie continued. "Was your son ever diagnosed with depression?"

"No, not formally, but like everyone, he got a little blue once in a while."

"Was he having trouble sleeping?"

"A little. Sometimes I'd look out the window and see the garage apartment light on late at night, but I figured he was studying. He's working on his GED in addition to working full time."

"Did he use drugs?"

"A long time ago. He's clean now."

"Did he ever—"

"Are you a mother?"

"Excuse me?"

Mrs. Brown leaned toward Lottie, the plastic tubing stretching and straining. "Do you have children, Detective King?"

Lottie stared at the scattered birthday cards but didn't see words or pictures. She saw bits and pieces of her own past. She'd been in Rowena Brown's shoes, but she didn't have a loved one headed to the morgue. Thank the Lord of all things great and small. "I have three girls," Lottie said softly.

"And you know things about your girls, right? Things other people would never know?"

Lottie knew when her oldest, Chantelle, a straight-A student, got a B plus on an exam. Her daughter would haul out the blender and make vanilla milkshakes with malted milk balls. She knew the day her middle daughter, Kass, had her first kiss. Kass held her hand to her cheek all weekend, a dreamy smile on her face. And she knew when little Tiarra broke the neighbor's window. Tee stuttered for two days until she fessed up. "Yes, Mrs. Brown, I know things about my girls."

"Because children share our bodies. They are conceived and grow just below our hearts." Mrs. Brown put the cards in a neat stack and set them in the box. "My son did not commit suicide, detective. My heart knows otherwise. Please keep me up to date on your investigation. I think you should start with that horrible man, Izzy Torino."

***

As Lottie headed down the Brown's front porch steps, a battered VW Bus with more primer than paint pulled up to the curb. A young man in a crisp white shirt and pleated black pants hurried up the walk. "Is Mrs. Brown inside?" he asked.

"And you are?"

"Corey Rhodes, from Mrs. Brown's church." He ran a hand over his short-cropped brown hair. "We just got word of Chickie's death, and I've come to pray with her."

"You knew Chickie?"

"I'm the youth pastor, and at his mother's request I've been ministering to Chickie since he got out of prison. Now if you'll excuse me, I need to tend to Mrs. Brown. She's been a big supporter of our youth program, and I want to support her in her time of need." He tried to shoot past Lottie, but she grabbed his arm.

"When was the last time you saw Chickie?"

"Friday night."

Lottie released his arm but moved to the middle of the walk, blocking his way. "Where?"

With an irritated sigh, Corey Rhodes added, "I visited him at his garage apartment. Chickie had promised to be at a youth group fundraiser for our new bus, but he and the money he raised didn't show up. I'm not going to lie. I thought the worst. Chickie was a known thief, and he told me pointblank he thought his mom was a fool for spending so much time and what little money she had on our ministries." The hard lines around the youth minister's mouth softened and turned down. "When I got here, he was sitting on the bed and holding his gun. He'd been crying."

"Do you know why?"

"Chickie had met with Mrs. Brown's doctor that morning, and the doc said the cancer had spread to her liver and pancreas. She had less than a month to live. Chickie blamed himself. He said his mom always worried about him, and when she was worried, she smoked like a chimney. He said he deserved to die, not his mom. We talked about how devastated she'd be if something happened to Chickie, and by the time I left, he realized killing himself was stupid and selfish."

"Chickie and his mom were close?"

"Chickie's father took off when Chickie was a baby, so his mom raised him. Chickie had been in denial about the whole cancer thing, but after the meeting with the doctor, Chickie couldn't pretend she was going to get better." The young man straightened his cuffs. "If you're done with your questions, I need to tend to a dying woman."

The sun had dropped below the horizon, but a soft peachy glow still clung to the sky. As the minister went inside the Brown house, Lottie parked her hiney on the porch and settled the clipboard on her lap, making notes on her discussions with Corey Rhodes and Mrs. Brown.

The radio at her waist squawked. It was one of the crew from the crime lab. There were no superstars in police work. Picture a giant constellation of men and women holding up tiny candles to shine the light on justice: patrol officers, detectives, and crime–scene techs who didn't carry guns but magnifying glasses.

"Got a match for you, Lottie," one of the experts from latent told her over the radio. "The prints found on the gun match Chickie Brown's."

Check.

A tech from ballistics chimed in, "The bullet that killed Chickie Brown came from a nine millimeter just like the one you found on the garage floor."

Check.

Of course there was the locked room. That was a gargantuan checkmark.

According to the mounting evidence, the victim was also the killer.

My son did not commit suicide. My heart knows otherwise.

Unfortunately, broken hearts weren't too reliable.

Lottie tucked her pen behind her right ear. Something else was niggling at her, that big box of cards.

A curl of smoke tickled her nose, followed by the words, "You're thinking."

Lottie turned to her boss and mentor, Sergeant Gorman, who was coming up the walk. "And you're smoking. Your wife's gonna kill you."

"If the cancer sticks don't first."

"Either way, when you're gone I call dibs on your snazzy lumbar support chair."

With a half laugh, Sergeant Gorman tossed the half-smoked cigarette onto the ground and ground it with his boot heel. He stuck a matchstick in the corner of his mouth and held out his hand. She handed him her notes, and he flipped through the pages. "Suicide?"

"Not sure."

"Tell me about it." The matchstick started a slow amble across his lips.

"The mom insists he wasn't capable of suicide."

"Lottie..."

"And the kid bought his dying mother soup but didn't give it to her."

"Lottie, you're a smart cop, and I'll bet the bank that you're going to be one of the finest homicide detectives ever to beat the streets of Colorado Springs. The thing is, you also have a big heart, which is going to serve you well because with big hearts come big passions. But that big heart can get you in trouble. Brown's mother, she got to you, and the one thing you have to remember is grieving family members are not reliable witnesses."

"So let's take the mother's testimony out of it and"— Lottie held up the bag with the suicide note—"focus on this."

The matchstick stopped mid–shuffle. "You doubting its authenticity?"

"I compared the handwriting on the suicide note to the handwriting in his address book and the cards he wrote to his mother. They're the same. The mother agreed."

"Then what's niggling at you?"

***

Present Day

Every girl in the Girl Power circle sat on the edge of her sit-upon, eyes wide.

"Well?" Aitana demanded.

Lottie waved the lightning rod at the circle of girls. "You tell me."

Markayla shot her hand in the air in one of those pick-me, pick-me waves. "Yes, Markayla."

"It's how he signed his name."

Hot dang! Lottie loved this kid.

***

'bout Thirty Years Ago

"Chickie isn't something I'd want to name the grandson," Sergeant Gorman said. "But it's the name he uses everywhere. Job applications. Note to his girlfriend."

"But not with his mom," Lottie insisted. "Rowena Brown hated her son's street name. Always referred to him as Benjamin. Did you see all of those birthday cards? All signed Benjamin with a heart over the *j*. So if he wrote a suicide note to his mother, one meant to put her at ease and show his love until they saw each other in the next world, he would have signed it Benjamin, not Chickie."

Gorman's matchstick made another round trip. "The only prints on the gun belonged to Brown."

"I know."

"Gun was fired at close range."

"I know."

"Brown presented with suicidal indicators."

"I know."

"And you got that locked room."

"I know." She pressed her hands into the sides of her head. "You gonna make me close the case?"

"I'm giving you until eight in the morning. That gives you fourteen hours."

Lottie looked at her watch. "And seven minutes."

Chapter Three

Good homicide detectives were like hungry dogs. They never gave up the bone. They kept gnawing and grinding until something broke and they reached the juicy, meaty center.

The problem was Lottie had that darned locked room and was having a dickens of a time figuring out *how* anyone but Chickie Brown could have pulled that trigger. With the clock ticking, she needed to give up that bone and find another. Chewing on the *who* and *why* might get her more meat.

She needed to find out who wanted Chickie Brown dead and why? And since dead bodies and smoking guns weren't good conversationalists, she needed people. Lottie took out Watson's list of witnesses.

Maralee Frye and her son, Jackson, lived next door and were the ones who helped Brown's mother break into the locked garage.

"How's Rowena holding up?" Maralee Frye ushered Lottie into her kitchen where she was tossing tiny egg-shaped dumplings into a large pot of simmering broth. "I'm making her soup."

"Mrs. Brown's a strong woman," Lottie said. "A

pastor from her church is with her now."

"I can't imagine what that must have been like, finding your son dead." Her eyes misted as she dusted flour from her hands. "What can I help you with, Detective King?"

"Did you see anyone near the Brown's garage this afternoon between ten and noon?"

"No one."

"How about in the neighborhood? Did you see any strange cars or unfamiliar people?"

The older woman's fingers tightened around the soup spoon. "Unfortunately, all the time. People are always driving along this street, hoping to score a bit of something. As you know, this is a rough neighborhood, which is why I'm glad my son will be getting out soon."

"Where is Jackson?" This was the kid who broke the window and busted into the garage.

"In his room. This whole thing's been hard on him."

Lottie found Jackson Frye in a back bedroom sitting at a desk with a thick textbook cracked open, but he wasn't reading. Instead, he stared out the window. Unblinking. Motionless.

"You and Chickie were close?" Lottie asked.

Jackson jumped and ran the back of his hand across his eyes. Then he shrugged. "Not really. We didn't hang out with the same crowd at school." Jackson Frye was the antithesis of Chickie Brown. Neatly trimmed hair. No tats or fancy jewelry. Label-free jeans. Room sparse but clean.

"You were next door neighbors for most of your lives," Lottie added. "You must have hung out together in the summers or when you were younger."

Another shrug.

This kid was going to be a tough nut to crack. "What did you guys do for fun?"

"Stuff."

Lottie ran her hand over the patched seat of a ten-speed bike tucked behind the door. "Did you ride bikes? Go fishin'? Play video games?"

The kid shook his head. "Neither one of us had a lot of stuff when we were kids. You know. Single moms. No money." A hint of a smile cracked the somber plane of his face. "But, yeah, we had fun. Chickie always came up with crazy stuff to do. We'd build forts with boxes we found behind the grocery store and catch bullfrogs down at the creek. Chickie loved animals. One time we taught a stray dog how to jump through old tires and pull a flag down on the mailbox. Fun stuff. Little kid stuff."

"Sounds like Chickie Brown was a friend."

"I guess he was."

"Until he joined up with Izzy Torino."

Jackson's face hardened. "Chickie changed after that. Suddenly he had *stuff*. New bike. Tricked-out stereo system. Air Jordans."

"Not your cuppa?"

"What Chickie spent on clothes last year would pay for a semester worth of books at college."

Lottie motioned to the stack of books on the desk. "You plan on going to college?"

"If I get enough scholarships." He rested his hand on a thick calculus book.

Lottie dipped her head at the window, which overlooked the Frye backyard and part of the Brown's backyard. "You see anyone around the garage today?"

The boy tore his gaze from the window, his face lined in confusion. "My mom said Chickie left behind a suicide note. You think someone killed him?"

"We're just covering all the bases. Did you see anyone near the garage anytime today?"

Jackson shook his head. "I've been at work all day. My shift at the gas station was from eight to four."

Lottie pointed to the clear view of the Brown's garage apartment. "With a view like this, I'm sure you've seen stuff. Before you went to work? Yesterday? Earlier in the week?"

The kid stared at his sneakers. Off-brand. Two neighbor boys from a rough part of town with two very different lives.

"Jackson?" Lottie prompted.

"To earn some extra cash, I do yard work for people in the neighborhood, including Mrs. Brown, and a few times while I was over there, I saw some people go into Chickie's place."

"People?"

"I didn't recognize them."

"But you saw what they were doing?"

"Yeah. I didn't want his mom to find out because it would kill her. Mrs. Brown thinks Chickie got himself straightened out."

"But..."

"For the past few weeks I've seen deals going down. Chickie's selling again."

"Any problems with deals? Any angry customers?"

"Not that I saw."

"Do you know of anyone who wanted Chickie dead?"

"Like I said, I didn't hang out with Chickie or any of his friends. Sorry, but I need to get back to studying."

And Lottie needed to get back to digging up more bones.

***

Izzy Torino had a pug nose, and tonight it was blue.

Lottie tossed a photo of Chickie Brown on the pool table at the Balls & Brew pool hall off Academy. "You know this guy?"

Torino tapped the photo with his cue stick then turned to Lottie, his gaze pausing at her chest. "Nope."

Lottie jammed her arms over her chest. "Do I look stupid?"

"You look hot." The tip of his cue stick followed the curve of Lottie's legs and came to rest near her shoe. "Nice hooves."

She kicked the wooden stick. "Keep it up and you're getting a hoof up your hind end."

"Ooooo, I like my women with a little kick."

"Then answer my question, Torino." She aimed her chin at the photo. "Do you know this man? And just so you know, I found your name and phone number in his address book."

"What an idiot." Torino picked up a small square of blue chalk and rubbed it on the tip of his cue stick. "Sure. I know Chickie."

"Friends? Bowling buddy? Pool pal?"

"Chickie Brown is a business associate, and just so *you* know, I do business with a lot of people."

"You won't be doing anymore with Chickie." She took out the Polaroid of Brown's dead body.

The stick slipped from Torino's hand, clattering to the greasy linoleum floor. A second later, Torino rubbed his forehead and gave an exaggerated wince. "Ouch. Must have hurt." Smart aleck.

"Where were you between ten and noon today?" Lottie asked.

Torino picked up his stick. "Where I am every Sunday. In church."

"Yeah, right."

"I'm dead serious." Torino made prayer hands around the stick. "Ask my pastor. I stuck around after services and served donuts."

That didn't mean this guy wasn't guilty. He ran a drug machine and had plenty of moving parts—or in this case, people—at his beck and call. "Who does your dirty work?"

"You're barking up the wrong tree, pit bull. I did not kill Chickie Brown." The cocky grin slipped away. "He..."

"He what?"

"Chickie Brown was one of my most successful business associates, a guy who knew how to grow an opportunity. You don't reward that kind of talent with a pop to the head." Izzy Torino met her gaze head-on, daring her to call him a liar.

She couldn't. According to the team from narc, Izzy Torino was a drug-dealing streak on dirty underwear, but he was also a businessman. He was all about the money, and if Brown was bringing in the green, then Torino wouldn't call for a hit. "But I'm in the forest, aren't I? Chickie Brown's death had something to do with your meth operation."

Torino laughed. "Do *I* look stupid?"

Lottie plucked a napkin from a dispenser on the bar and swiped the blue chalk from his nose. "Yeah, you do."

***

Midnight had come and gone, and Lottie was back in Chickie Brown's garage apartment. The coroner's office had transported Brown's body to the morgue, but everything else remained the same. Moldy olives sat next to a fresh cup of chicken tortilla soup. Crunchy critter droppings surrounded a whiz-bang television. Spider webs still clung to that darned locked door.

She, on the other hand, had changed. She now knew Chickie was dealing and working for Izzy Torino. Same old evidence, but this time viewed with new eyes.

Once again, she walked the garage apartment, stopping in all four corners and taking a mental snapshot. She poked under the bed and opened drawers. At the nightstand drawer, she paused and pulled out the map. It was a city street map, and someone, presumably Chickie, had run a highlighter down random streets in different colors. This time she noticed small symbols: one handwritten dollar sign next to yellow streets, two dollar signs next to blue streets, and three dollar signs next to green streets.

My most successful business associate, Torino had said. And how do you reward a business associate? More business, or in this case, more territory. Chickie Brown's territory was growing, which could mean that another associate's territory was shrinking.

Young Watson, a steamy cup of coffee in each hand, poked his head through the doorway. "Thought you might need this. It's getting late." For him, too. He'd been the first responder and could have clocked out hours ago. "Want me to get you a burger or something?"

Time to reward good work. "I'm not hungry, but thanks. You find anything?" She took the coffee from his hand and invited him inside.

With the eagerness of a pup, Watson whipped out his pocket-size notebook. "I followed up with the call center Chickie Brown told his mom he was working for. Turns out he was there three days and quit. Said he couldn't work for the chump change they were paying him."

"Which is probably when he went back to work for Izzy Torino." After a long draw of coffee, she studied the highlighted city map still in her hand. "When I interviewed Torino I got the impression he knows who wanted Brown dead, but he won't hand over any names, which makes me think it wasn't a competitor or customer but someone in Torino's organization."

"Why would someone on Torino's team want Chickie Brown dead?"

"Territory. I'm thinking Brown's a casualty of a turf war."

Watson studied the map. "We need to find out who was working these areas before Brown got out of jail."

"Exactly. Time to hit the streets." Again she looked around the room, her gaze landing on the refrigerator. "But first we're heading to Taco Tilly's."

"I thought you weren't hungry."

"Not for tacos." She had her eye on another bone.

***

"According to the deputy coroner," Lottie said as Watson pulled his cruiser into one of the two spaces that served as Taco Tilly's parking lot, "Brown died between ten and noon. Since Brown purchased the chicken tortilla soup at nine, one of the last people to see him alive was the person who sold him the soup."

"You think maybe Chickie was working a deal here?" Watson turned off the engine.

Taco Tilly's was a twenty-four-hour Mexican food restaurant, the kind with mismatched chairs, chipped tables, paper plates, and a small but authentic menu. It was also just a half-mile from the Brown house and catered to, as Maralee Frye said, a "rough crowd."

"I'm thinking a kid who just bought his dying mother soup didn't plan on dying himself."

The clerk at the all-night take-out counter said the owner, Tilly, ran the morning shift on Sunday, and she was in the back preparing carnitas.

"Do you recognize this man?" Lottie flashed Chickie Brown's mug shot at Tilly, who was up to her elbows in chopped onions.

The restaurant owner set down her knife and wiped the tears from her eyes with her shoulder. "Yes, he's come by a few times in the last couple of months. Always buys a family size serving of soup."

"When was the last time you saw him?"

"Yesterday morning. Our soup special was menudo, but he wanted the chicken tortilla soup. Said it was for a sick relative."

"What was his state of mind?"

"Tired. I got the impression he'd been working all night and was on his way home." From peddling drugs. Yet here he was doing something nice for his dying mother.

"Was anyone with him?"

"Not with him, but he was talking to another guy in the parking lot. They were arguing. The other guy kept getting in your guy's face and poking his finger at his chest. He was riled up. Ready to kill."

"Did they come to blows?"

"No. Your guy's order was up. He took the soup and left."

"What did the other man look like?"

"Youngish. Short brown hair. Real clean-cut."

***

Present Day

"It was the pastor!" Aitana.

"No, Jackson Frye, the boy next door." Julia.

"They both have short brown hair and are clean-cut." Natalee.

"It could be either one." Brooke Lynn.

Lottie held up her index finger. "Not everything

about them was the same."

Quiet settled in. Lottie could hear the gears in their heads turning, the brain cells whirring.

"Their wheels." Markayla's excited voice broke the silence. "The pastor drove an old VW Bus, and Jackson rode an old bike."

Lottie grinned. This little gal was going to be heading up the FBI in a decade or two.

***

'bout Thirty Years Ago

Lottie pictured two clean cut-men: the youth pastor and the young neighbor. "How did the other young man get to the restaurant?"

"He rode a bike."

***

"I need to talk to you about the murder of Chickie Brown," Lottie told a yawning Jackson Frye who'd just stumbled out of bed and stood on his front porch. With his sleep-rumpled hair and ratty T-shirt, he didn't look so clean-cut now.

"I told you everything I know," Jackson said.

"Then let me tell you what *I* know. In my line of work there's this thing called MMO: motive, means, and opportunity. And when folks in my world are tracking down and prosecuting criminals, those three little letters are important."

"What are you talking about?"

"Your involvement in Chickie's murder."

A barely-there tremor rocked his hand as he pushed back the hair hanging over his forehead.

"I'm not sure what you're getting at Detective King, I'm one of the good ones."

"No one is all good or bad. It's part of being human," Lottie went on. "As for motive, you, Jackson, had a good reason to kill Chickie Brown. You need money for college, and despite working two jobs—at the gas station and doing yard work for neighbors—you were falling short, so you went to work for Izzy Torino."

This time a tremor shook Jackson's entire body. "You can't prove that." He swatted at the air, as if dealing with an annoying mosquito.

"No, but I'm sure we can get someone from Izzy's crew, maybe even Izzy himself, to turn on you."

His eyes shifted, the gaze sharpening and hardening. He was still the kid who dreamed of a better life through books and scholarships, but he was also a kid who would do anything to make that dream a reality, including murder. "Who's a judge and jury going to believe?" Jackson rested his fingertips on his chest and smiled. "An honors student with two jobs or a bunch of street thugs who deal drugs?"

"Then we get to means," Lottie continued, her teeth clamped around that bone. "You, Jackson, had the ability to commit the crime. You live next door, and because you do yard work for Mrs. Brown, you've been around and in the garage. You could have easily gone through Chickie's nightstand drawer and knew about the gun."

Jackson leaned against the door frame and yawned.

"I'm tired, so please get this over with. I believe we're on the letter O."

"I'll admit, you got me there. I can't figure out how you got in and out of that locked room to kill Chickie Brown." She inched closer. "Care to tell me?"

"I already told you, Detective King, I was gone all day, working from eight to four, pumping gas and washing windows. I never left the gas station. You can ask the assistant manager who was running the cash register."

Lottie knotted her hands behind her back so she didn't let a clenched fist fly and pop the smirk off Jackson Frye's face. She took one more step toward him, so close she could see grains of sleepy sand at the corners of his eyes. "I know you killed him, Jackson Frye."

Wrapping a yawn around a smile, he shrugged. "And I know you can't prove it."

Chapter Four

In police investigations, every once in a great while a blue bird, otherwise known as an unexpected clue or witness, flew in and gave the investigator that little bit of something that would help break a case wide open.

Lottie looked at her hands. Empty. No blue feather or even a smear of bird poop.

It was almost eight o'clock Monday morning, and while she was ready to point the finger at neighbor boy Jackson Frye for the murder of his drug dealer competitor, Chickie Brown, she couldn't figure out how he did it. Darn that locked room.

She stopped by the morgue to see the Great Dondini zipping up the bag that held the earthly remains of Benjamin "Chickie" Brown.

"Pull any rabbits out of your hat on this one?" Lottie asked.

"No rabbits but a *rattus norvegicus*."

"Excuse me?"

"I found some hair on Brown's body inconsistent with his own. Turned out to be hair from a rat."

Lottie pictured all those critter droppings and that long, scaly tail. "Makes sense. That garage he lived in is full of pests." She shivered. Then froze.

Incoming! She just got her a bluebird.

***

Present Day

"Huh?"

"I don't get it."

"A rat?"

"A bluebird?"

"What does all of this have to do with Chickie Brown's murder?"

As the girls in the Girl Power circle talked over one another, Lottie took the lightning rod from her back pocket and studied the bits of silver glitter.

Bella aimed an accusing finger at Lottie. "You can't leave us hanging."

"Sure I can." Lottie rolled the rod back and forth on her hand, the garage light overhead sending bits of light through the Girl Power circle. According to the Girl Power Guidebook, whoever held the lightning rod had the opportunity to speak. It was a great way to corral chaos and make sure every girl had a chance to be heard. Such a simple device, but powerful. Man, she wished she'd had something like this when dealing with folks at crime scenes, not to mention courtrooms.

The girls continued to talk, their voices and the chaos growing.

Markayla's fingers twitched, and slowly she extended her hand. A slight tremor rocked her fingers. Uncertainty? Excitement? Probably a bit of both. Even after thousands of cases, Lottie still got that feeling. With a grave nod, Lottie held out the lightning rod.

Markayla wrapped her fingers about metal. The circle fell silent. Markayla took a deep breath. "Chickie Brown's killer was a rat."

"As in a bad guy?" Brooke Lynn asked.

"No, as in a *rat* rat."

***

'bout Thirty Years Ago

Watson pulled his cruiser onto the sidewalk in front of the Frye house, blocking Jackson Frye as he peddled down the driveway, a loaded book bag perched on his back.

Lottie stepped out of the cruiser. "We need to talk to you about the murder of Chickie Brown."

Jackson extended his legs, stopping the bike before he ran into the cruiser. "Let's try this one last time, Detective King. I was at work all day yesterday. I was never in Chickie Brown's apartment. I never touched that gun."

"True. You didn't pull the trigger on the gun that killed Chickie Brown, but you know the rat that did. As a matter of fact, you taught him—or her—how to do it."

"You're crazy."

"Like a fox." This time it was Lottie who wore a smug grin. "Or should we say *rattus norvegicus*, also known as a common brown rat, which for those in the know are intelligent, good with humans, and trainable."

Jackson picked at the ragged tape on the curved handlebar of his ten-speed.

"Chickie ran with a rough crowd, so rough he felt the

need to sleep with a gun next to his bed," Lottie said. "Everyone knew that, including you. You and Chickie were resourceful young kids with not a lot of money but plenty of imagination. You probably trained a rat or two in your day, just like you trained that dog."

Jackson's other hand clawed at the tape on the other handlebar. *Scritch. Scritch.*

"So you taught the rat how to pull the trigger of the gun, using bits of dried cereal as rewards. When your rat assassin was ready, you positioned the gun on Chickie's nightstand at the height and angle that would land a bullet in his head."

"Chickie wrote a suicide note. It was his handwriting."

"Yep. That one had me stumped until I remembered Chickie's pastor said he was pretty broken up on Friday after learning of his mom's eminent death. He blamed himself. Said he should be dead instead. I'm thinking he wrote the note but you signed his name."

"Thinking and proving are two different things." Jackson's knuckles grew white as he gripped the handlebars tighter.

"Yep, and that's why I had the guys in latent check the pen found with the suicide note in Chickie's nightstand drawer. They found a set of fingerprints that did not belong to Chickie. Right now those prints are being checked against the ones found on the locked door. Yours."

Not everyone was all bad. Just like not everyone was all good. Time proved otherwise. Lottie checked her watch. It was one minute to eight.

Jackson's head rolled forward, his chin landing just above his heart. "I signed his name."

"Jackson Frye, you're under arrest for the murder of Chickie Brown."

Chapter Five

"That was the best meeting." Bella placed the last two cookies on a small plate. "Ever."

"Because you happen to have the best Girl Power troop." Lottie put the lightning rod back in her purse. "Ever." If Lottie could ever stop putting in sixty-hour workweeks, she'd sign on as co-leader of the Girl Power troop. She had a lot of miles on her high heels and plenty of life lessons to go with 'em. She reached for the greasy pan that had held the chicken wings.

Bella waved her off. "I got it, Grandma. I'm this week's meeting hostess, and it's my job."

That's another thing Lottie loved about this Girl Power troop business. The girls did some kick-butt activities and had a heck of a lot of fun, but they were also charged with the not-so-fun stuff, like clean-up.

Bella placed a leftover chicken wing on the plate with the cookies then slipped the greasy pan into the sink. "The snack was great and so was the investigation stuff." Bella scrubbed the pan. "I loved learning how to lift fingerprints and what coroners do. BTW, Markayla said she wants to take a fieldtrip to a morgue."

Lottie settled herself on a kitchen barstool. "Your

Girl Power troop wants to visit a morgue?"

"Markayla does. The rest of us will wait in the waiting room for her."

Another reason to love this Girl Power stuff. They supported one another. Every girl needed a pal or two at her side. Like her long-time friend, Ruthie Kells. Man, Lottie missed her friend, wished she'd spent more time with her before her death. "I'll talk to the Great Dondini and set something up."

Bella dried the pan. "I also like how you snuck in those lessons about drugs and smoking and how to tell if a friend is suicidal. Important stuff. But most of all, I loved how you solved the mystery in the locked room." Bella wiped down the counters. "Really amazing, Grandma, considering it all came down to a rat." With the kitchen sparkling, Bella hung up her towel. "But I won't tell anyone the whole thing was a lie."

Lottie wobbled on her stool. "A lie?"

"Come on, Grandma. You know we're smart. You tell us that all the time." Bella plopped her elbows on the kitchen counter and leaned toward Lottie, adding in a hushed voice. "There was no body in a locked room, no rat that pulled the trigger, no murder vic named Chickie Brown." Bella tilted her head to the plate holding what was left of their meeting snack: two brown butter salted caramel snickerdoodles and a chicken wing.

By golly, if she didn't have the most brilliant grandchildren on the planet.

Brown Butter Salted Caramel Snickerdoodles

Sweet and salty with a gooey center and a cinnamon kick!

Yield: Two dozen cookies; Prep time: 1 hour and 15 minutes; Total time: 1 hour 30 minutes

Ingredients
1 cup unsalted butter, sliced
2 1/2 cups all-purpose flour
1 teaspoon baking soda
2 teaspoons cream of tartar
1/2 teaspoon ground cinnamon
1/4 teaspoon sea salt
1 1/4 cups dark brown sugar
1/2 cup granulated sugar
1 large egg
1 egg yolk
2 teaspoons vanilla extract
1 tablespoon plain Greek yogurt
1 cup caramel squares, cut in half
For rolling the cookie dough:
1/4 cup granulated sugar
2 teaspoons ground cinnamon
Sea salt for topping cookies

Directions

1. Place sliced butter in heavy-bottomed saucepan and cook over medium heat, whisking often until it turns brown and you smell a nice, nutty aroma. Set aside to cool.

2. Whisk flour, baking soda, cream of tartar, cinnamon, and sea salt in a medium mixing bowl and set aside.

3. In a large mixing bowl, cream together the browned butter and sugars. Beat in egg, egg yolk, vanilla extract, and Greek yogurt. Mix in dry ingredients until just combined.

4. Form the dough into a large ball, cover tightly with plastic wrap, and place in refrigerator for 30 minutes.

5. Pre-heat oven to 350 degrees.

6. Divide and measure chilled dough into one tablespoon portions, and roll each into a ball. Flatten balls with palm and place two caramel halves onto each circle. Tuck dough around caramel and roll into a smooth ball again.

7. Mix 1/4 cup sugar and 2 teaspoons ground cinnamon in a small bowl. Roll dough balls in sugar mixture and place on baking sheet. Sprinkle with sea salt.

8. Bake cookies for 8-10 minutes until brown around the edges but still soft in the center and there are cracks on the surface of the cookie. Allow cookies to cool 2-3 minutes on the baking sheet. Transfer to wire rack and let cool.

Recipe adapted from Two Peas and Their Pod

Author's Note: When I was young, my mother worked in a library, and once a week she'd bring home an armload of cookbooks. Even as I child, I was an avid foodie, and I'd sit with my mom at the kitchen table reading those cookbooks like most teens would linger over *Tiger Beat* and *Seventeen Magazine*. It must be something in the genes, because my youngest daughter loves to read cookbooks and food blogs. She's also the family's finest baker and regularly makes these snickerdoodles, which are always a huge hit with family and her friends.

As a side note, my three girls grew up with "small furry rodents that are intelligent and particularly good with young children". That was the term I used when the girls first got their rats because I couldn't bring myself to use the words "pet" and "rat" in the same sentence. Initially, the girls wanted hamsters, but my husband did Internet research and discovered rats were much better pets. My girls named their new pets Choco, Chip, and Cookie. My oldest taught her rat, Choco, tricks, including how to jump from her head and onto the bed using bits of cereal. But can a rat really pull a trigger? Check the Internet. :-) Enjoy!

From the creative kitchen of award-winning author
Shelley Coriell
www.shelleycoriell.com

OLD FLAME

A Detective Lottie King Mystery

Chapter One

"Hey, Grandma," eleven-year-old Jeremy Jr. called out. "Gotta bullet for you. Go long."

Lottie King kicked off her ostrich skin mules and hauled ass across the backyard, zigging around the old peach tree and snagging the football out of the sweet morning air. "Outstanding pass, Jay-Jay. You'll make a fine NFL quarterback, that is, after you get your Ph.D. and discover the cure for cancer."

Bella, her twelve-year-old granddaughter, popped her head out the kitchen doorway. "I thought he was going to win the Nobel Peace Prize."

"Nope, that's your job." Lottie steadied herself against a low-hanging peach tree branch and sucked in a ragged breath. She really needed to take off a pound or twenty. "You got your homework done, young lady?"

"Not yet." Bella held up her hand before Lottie could shoot her the evil eye. "Doorbell rang. Someone needs to talk to you. He says it's an emergency."

"Tell him to call the police."

"Grandma, you *are* the police."

Lottie worked homicide for Colorado Springs PD, and she hadn't had a full day off in three months. Bad guys couldn't get their thick skulls around that whole I-need-a-day-off-to-rest-my-tired-feet thing. But after that business with the Broadcaster Butcher three months ago, she needed a break, a single day where Big Bads ceased to exist. Lottie shifted the football behind her right ear. "Tell him to visit me at work tomorrow." Which is when she'd be back at the best job in the world: catching killers.

Bella's freckled nose scrunched. "Are you sure? The kid looks upset."

"A kid?" Lottie dug her fingers into the pigskin. A *kid*. She tossed the ball to Jay-Jay. "Back in a flash."

The boy on her front porch was eleven, twelve tops, and he stood stone still but for the trembling of his lower lip. "Good morning, Sergeant King." He extended his hand. "I'm Gilbert James the Third."

"Gilbert James?" Lottie scratched at the curl that escaped the knot at the back of her head. Why did that name ring a bell?

The boy offered her a grave nod. "The Third."

And why did he look so familiar? Black-rimmed glasses, knobby knees, and a bushy head of coal-black hair. Lottie shook his hand. Ice-cold fingers, too. "Have we met before, Mr. Third?"

"No, but you knew"—a tremor rocked his jaw—"I mean, *know*, my granddaddy. You went to school with him. Gilbert James, the first one."

Gil? From high school? He was the bookish kid at the back of the class. Glasses. Tall. And that hair. A glorious lion's mane of ebony. "Gil," she said around an old smile. "How's your granddaddy these days?"

"He's missing." Tears flooded the boy's eyes and

spilled down his cheeks. "*And possibly dead.*"

***

Buttermilk-Crusted Blackberry Cobbler worked wonders, and by the time Little Gil finished a bowl, Lottie was happy to see the berries had done their job. No more tears.

"You want another?" Lottie asked just to be sure.

"No thank you, ma'am." The boy set his fork on the table and folded his hands in his lap. "But I need your help. I'd like to hire you to find my granddaddy."

Lottie sat on the kitchen chair next to the boy's. "You said your granddaddy's missing?" And possibly dead. She'd raised enough kids of her own and was in the throes of grandparenthood to know a child's imagination was a powerful thing, creating imaginary friends, magic kingdoms, and monsters under the bed.

"Yes, ma'am. Granddaddy left on Monday for another road trip. He has this new bike. Well, it's really an old bike, a 1926 Harley, but it's new to him, and boy, is it sa—weet. Cherry red with gold flame striping. Engine with twelve-hundred CCs." The kid must have realized he was smiling, and he dropped his gaze to the empty cobbler bowl.

"When was your granddaddy supposed to be back?"

"Next week."

She settled a hand on his arm until he looked at her. "So why all the fuss, son?"

"My birthday was yesterday, and he didn't call. Granddaddy never missed my birthday. Even if he was busy at work or at the hospital with grandma, he called. Always. Something happened to him."

"Have your parents filed a missing persons report?"

"No. I called the police, and they won't do anything, either." That little lip trembled again. "Something's wrong. Granddaddy would never forget my birthday."

A hand, no bigger than a baby's, touched her heart. Lottie knew first-hand the special connection between grandparents and their grands, but that wasn't tugging at her now. The fear and worry etched on this kid's face were just as visible as the streaks of dried tears. Real or imagined, this boy had a terrifying monster under his bed. Lucky for him that thirty-seven years ago she joined Colorado Springs PD intent on taking down monsters.

Lottie flexed her tired feet and hauled herself out of the chair. Some day she'd get a day off. "I'll take the case."

"You will?" The boy's eyes lit up for a fraction of a second before his face grew somber. "Um, what do you charge?"

This was one of them teaching moments. Kids—hell, everyone—needed to be held accountable for what they did and didn't do in this world, and if she was climbing out on a limb, Little Gil was coming with her. "Twenty dollars a day."

His teeth sank into his bottom lip.

She raised an index finger. "But a good thing for you, I'm running a half-price special."

The boy reached into the pocket of his jeans and pulled out a wad of crumpled dollar bills. He counted out nine and dug into his other pocket, pulling out two quarters, four dimes, and ten pennies. "You're hired."

***

"Really, Sergeant King, this is quite embarrassing." This from Gilbert James in the middle. "I'm afraid my son is wasting your time." Lottie stood in the middle of the James's living room, Little Gil's father looking distinctly uncomfortable and the kid looking at his dirty sneakers. "My father is in good health and loving life. Ever since he got that vintage Harley, he goes on these trips all the time. He'll ride days without checking in, and you know what? I'm happy for him. For more than forty years my dad chained himself to the desk of an accounting firm. He put two kids through college and supported my mother through five years of cancer and treatment before she died. Never spent a dime or time on himself. Then along came that old bike. He retired and got out more. Met new people. Saw new places. That bike changed him. Gave him the courage to leap."

"That's good to know, Mr. James, but my client has already paid for a full day of service, and I'm professionally obligated to investigate."

Gil Number Two grew thoughtful. "You know, my dad was sweet on you. Every time you appeared on the news about some police investigation, he said, *See Sergeant King there? That's my Lottie. First girl to ever steal my heart.*"

Lottie had occasionally talked to the shy, sweet boy at the back of the classroom, but back then she'd been blinded by Charles, who wasn't shy and, in the end, anything but sweet. "I never knew," Lottie said, surprised at the softness in her voice.

"Now you do, and when you find my dad, you two can catch up, maybe even rekindle an old flame." He winked.

Lottie almost laughed. The only flames she'd kindled the past few decades involved burning the midnight oil at her desk down at the station.

"I'm sure my father would love to see you, Sergeant King. So of course, I'll give you full cooperation with your *investigation*."

Ten minutes later Lottie sat in front of a computer in the James's kitchen, Little Gil still glued to her side. She'd learned Gil the First was last seen two days ago when he left for a scenic bike ride to Carlsbad, New Mexico.

"Everyone leaves a trail of some kind," Lottie told the boy as she reached for the mouse. "And credit cards are giant breadcrumbs. They tell us where people have been and what they were doing."

According to Gil's American Express card, her old schoolmate was having a raging love affair with motorcycles. Most of his purchases were from motorcycle shops, biker bars, and a leather retailer in Denver. He'd also forked over three hundred bucks at a toy store last week, and Lottie had a pretty good inkling Little Gil would be getting a mighty fine birthday present this year. On the day he left for the scenic ride, her old friend stopped at an ice cream shop in Alamosa in the early afternoon where he spent $4.64.

Hot fudge sundae. Extra walnuts.

Lottie blinked. Funny what was tucked in all those

old brain cells. Gil loved hot fudge sundaes with a double scoop of nuts. She remembered seeing him many times at the diner a block from the high school. One day she went to the diner to meet Charles but he'd stood her up. Gil, who must have noticed her sitting in the back booth more than a little perturbed, bought her a sundae and helped her with her math. Good guy. She was looking forward to reconnecting with him.

"Look here," she told Little Gil. "Your granddaddy arrived in Santa Fe Monday night. He bought gas, ate dinner, and stayed one night at a motel off Highway 285. Yesterday morning, he ate breakfast in a Santa Fe coffee shop and stopped by a Super Target. Last night he arrived in Cloudcroft, New Mexico, where he bought dinner at a restaurant called Eddie Ray's."

"And then?"

Nothing. No hotel charge for last night. No breakfast or lunch charge for today. She clicked the mouse and refreshed the page, but it remained empty. All activity stopped in Cloudcroft, a small mountain town just north of the Texas border. No more breadcrumbs.

Chapter Two

Cloudcroft, New Mexico, was seven and a half hours south of Colorado Springs. Despite the grumbling and groans from her old Jeep Cherokee, Lottie made it in six.

At nine-thousand feet above sea level, Cloudcroft was literally a town in the clouds, but there was nothing heavenly about Eddie Ray's. The biker bar off Burro Avenue smelled of greasy burgers, motor oil, and attitude.

With only two other diners in the restaurant, Lottie had her choice of seats. She sat at the bar and took out a picture of Gil on his bike. Her old classmate had aged well. He still had the nerdy glasses, sweet smile, and a head full of hair, although now gray and cropped close to his head. He wore full leathers, black and red, that showed a little bit of a gut. She wondered if he liked blackberry cobbler. Or peanut brittle. She made a mean peanut brittle, with peanuts, mind you, none of them pansy-ass macadamia nuts.

"Do you recognize this man?" Lottie asked the bartender, a small woman with long braids, faded green headband, and leather vest.

The bartender wiped the counter, her sun-roughened

skin stretching over bulging muscle. "You a cop?"

Lottie pictured the Glock and badge in her bag. Never left home without 'em. "An old friend."

The bartender tossed the towel over her shoulder and set a napkin in front of Lottie who ordered a long neck and the fish fry basket and ignored the nagging voice of her middle daughter who was always after her to eat foods like kale and Tofurkey.

"Your friend came in here last night right before we closed," the bartender said. "Nice guy. Sweet bike. Had everyone buzzing about it. We'd already closed the grill, so I served him a turkey club. Hunted down a slice of pie, too. He left me a ten-dollar tip. Like I said, nice guy."

"Did he have anything to drink?" Old Gil wouldn't be the first to tip back one too many and forget the date, including a grandson's birthday.

"Coke. Easy Ice."

"What time did he leave?"

"Straight up ten o'clock. He was the last one in the place. I'd finished my shift, so we walked out together."

"And then?"

"I got in my truck."

"And Gil?"

"He went to the hog rail and hopped on his bike." She rasped out a dry-leather laugh. "Man, you could tell he loved that bike. He stroked the case like he was stroking a woman in his bed."

"Did you see where he went?"

"Nope, I drove off, but he mentioned in the bar that he was bunking down for the night."

According to Mr. American Express Card, that didn't

happen. Of course Gil could have stayed with friends, but his son said he didn't have any in this area, and he wasn't a member of any bike club, either. Her old friend could have paid cash, but almost forty years in the trenches had taught her a thing or two about human nature. People were creatures of habit. Gil's traveling buddy was his AmEx card. Plus, Gil was a smart numbers guy, an accountant. He traveled on plastic. Safer. More convenient.

After downing the longneck and grease, Lottie went outside where the neon sign above the door cut through the gray dusk. Tonight two bikes stood at the wooden hog rail, horses with shiny paint and chrome. Squinting through the twilight, she studied the ground: big shoe prints, narrow tire tracks, two cigarette butts, and a wad of green gum. No signs of struggle. No blood. Not even any oil or fluid indicating recent mechanical issues.

So why the hell didn't Old Gil call Little Gil on his birthday? Why no more breadcrumbs from the AmEx card? What happened to Gil James after he got on his bike last night right at this spot?

Lottie jammed a hand into her bag. With all the shit she carried in her purse, she could survive the Apocalypse. At last she unearthed a flashlight. She swiped the light across the shadowed side of the railing. After poking around here, she'd head to local motels and—

The light stilled on a spot of red. She squatted, her knees creaking. Up close she could see a red slash along the bottom half of the railing. She ran her finger over the red paint with a sliver of gold.

***

Back in the bar, a beefy guy with a baby face and bushy head of brown hair sat on the barstool next to Lottie. Eddie Ray, the bar owner, reminded her of a giant teddy bear.

She handed him Gil's photo. "Guy named Gil James. Rode in here last night on a vintage bike."

The bar owner scratched his furry chin. "Doesn't look familiar."

"According to the bartender, Gil was your last customer of the night," Lottie prompted.

"Yeah, I remember now. Turkey club and apple pie, but I didn't see him. By that time I was in the back mopping floors."

"What time did you leave?"

"Got receipts tallied, toilets scrubbed, and everything shut down around ten thirty."

"Did you see Mr. James in the parking lot?"

"Nope. Not a living soul around."

Lottie fished from her bag a Hello Kitty pen and notebook, gifts from one of the grands on her birthday last year. "Any other people in the bar last night when Mr. James arrived?"

"Other than the bartender, there was Ricco, the dishwasher, and a few regulars. A couple that run the gift shop next door came in for a late dinner. Tolliver was here, too." The bar owner's lip curled in a snarl.

"Tolliver?"

"Scumbag druggie who just got out on parole. Busted for dealing. Right here in my place. Bad for my bottom line. Lost a lot of business that week."

Which was nothing like losing a granddaddy.

***

Ricco, a twenty-something with greased back hair and a scorpion tattooed on his neck, stood at a giant dented sink, sliding congealed cheese from a plate.

Lottie flashed him Gil's photo. "You ever seen this guy?"

The plate slipped from his hand, and an arc of greasy water splashed his T-shirt. "No."

"Think harder," she said. "He was in here last night right before closing."

The kid dug through the chunky water, plates clanking. No eye contact. *Tsk. Tsk. Tsk.* Little boys who refused to look you in the eye were usually hiding something.

She jammed the photo under his nose. "Look closer."

Ricco craned his neck and shrugged. "Yep, I saw him. Killer bike."

Yeah, she got it. It was a sweet bike, but Gil was also a sweet grandfather who at one time had been sweet on her. Where the hell was this guy? "When did you last see him?"

"When I kicked off for the night, about nine thirty. Eddie Ray let me go early because it was a slow night, and he's always looking for ways to save a buck. I saw the old guy in the parking lot letting some gawkers take pictures."

She pictured that slash of red on the hog rail. "Any

damage to the bike?"

"Nope, perfect shape."

"Did he appear to be having any mechanical issues?"

"Cranked right up. Man the roar was beautiful."

"You haven't seen him since?"

The dishwasher finally looked her in the eye. "No."

Lottie tucked the photo into her bag and pulled out a business card. "In case you remember something, give me a call."

Ricco's fingers wrapped around the sponge, squeezing it dry. "You're...uh...a cop?"

"In this case, yes." She set the card next to a giant bottle of soap. "Does that change any of your answers?"

He turned his gaze back to the slick, gray water and scrubbed.

***

Outside the moon was high, the air cold. Nine-thousand feet above stress was Cloudcroft's motto. The main drag had a few nice shops, including a newer-looking biker bar and western wear shop with shoes in the window. After she found Gil, maybe she'd celebrate with a new pair of high-heeled boots.

Next door at the gift shop she caught the store owners just as they were locking up for the night.

"Sure we saw him last night," the owner said. "Gil was his name, right? What a bike. He let me take a picture of my wife, Millie, on it."

"Do you know where he was headed last night after dinner at Eddie Ray's?" Lottie asked.

"He was going to get a motel and some shut eye. We recommended the Cloud Top B&B. The innkeeper makes melt-in-your-mouth cinnamon rolls every morning. Plus they have great cell phone coverage."

"Oh, that's right," the wife said. "Your friend said he'd been trying to call his grandson all day because it was the boy's birthday, but he couldn't get any calls to go through. Bad reception."

No bars. Bingo! That's why Gil never called his grandson. It made sense. Except for the fact that most motels, hotels, or bed and breakfasts had at least one landline.

***

Lottie tapped the brake and eased around another switchback, her Jeep hugging the mountain as she inched along the road to the Cloud Top B&B. She squinted through the black night. Was that another turn? Lordy, it was like driving through ink. A soul not paying attention could end up plunging into the rocky canyon hundreds of feet below.

She took another turn. Rocks plinked the underbelly of her Jeep and trickled over the cliff into the blackened chasm. At last she reached the Cloud Top B&B.

"Yes, I was expecting Mr. James last night," the B&B owner said. "Marv and Millie from the Antlers Gift Shop phoned to tell me he was coming, but he never showed."

Her gut tightened. Had her old friend lost control of his bike or misjudged a turn? Had he roared off the edge and dropped into darkness?

"Is there anything else I can help you with, Sergeant King?"

Lottie steadied her feet and checked her watch. It was too late to head back to Colorado Springs, even though she had work tomorrow. She shifted from one denim stiletto to the other. She had a hell of a lot of vacation days racked up.

"I'd like a room," she told the B&B owner.

Once in the Cloud Three Suite, Lottie kicked off her shoes, the dangling cherries clinking as the stilettos fell to the floor. She powered up her cell phone, and within seconds, bars lit up its face followed by a series of sharp, loud dings. Cell coverage confirmed. There were twelve messages on her phone, ten from Little Gil, all begging her to call him ASAP.

"You were right, Sergeant King!" Little Gil said. "The credit card leaves behind breadcrumbs. A new charge appeared on Granddaddy's American Express account. He bought a leather jacket in El Paso yesterday. That means he's in El Paso, right?"

"Darned good possibility." She jotted down the retailer's name. Maybe Old Gil never drove up that twisting mountain road to the Cloud Top B&B. Maybe he damaged his bike at Eddie Ray's. Maybe he hobbled to El Paso, the closest big city, for repair work, and while in the big city, maybe he bought himself a fancy new jacket.

***

Armed with a cinnamon roll, Lottie headed back down the mountain the next morning and was in El Paso in an hour and a half where she stopped at Full Throttle, a biker bar with an attached retail shop, the same shop where Gil, or someone intimate with his American Express card, purchased a leather jacket two nights ago.

"Are you kidding, lady?" The store manager handed her back Gil's photo. "There's a bike rally this week, and we have extended hours and big crowds. You expect me to remember one customer?"

"He wasn't your typical customer. Grandfatherly type, soft-spoken, looked like a mild-mannered accountant."

"Doesn't ring a bell."

"He rides a 1926 Harley. Red and gold."

"Don't remember that, either."

Odd. That bike got noticed. She talked to the clerk who worked that night, but she didn't remember Old Gil or the Harley.

As Lottie made her way to the exit, she snaked through racks and stands of blingy biker gear: studded saddlebags, leather chaps, and silver boot chains. She fingered one of the tags. Pricey stuff.

She turned back to the manager. "Do you have security cameras in this place? Ones that work." Lottie always said that after she retired she'd write a how-to manual for Big Bads because boy did she have insider info, including the fact that while most retail shops these days had cameras, many were dummies or they didn't work. Lucky for her, Full Throttle had a shrinkage problem and just installed a shiny new video surveillance system that was fully functioning.

Ten minutes later, Lottie sat in the manager's office

going through security footage. Lots of leather and sun-baked skin. Old and young and everyone in between. In the footage from two nights ago, a figure with a leather jacket that matched the one Gil James bought popped onto the monitor, and she froze the frame. A young man stood at the checkout counter, his face turned away from the camera, but there was something about him. She zoomed in and frowned. Then she checked the time stamp. Almost one in the morning. The timing *could* work.

The cherries on her heels tinkling, she pressed a button and took a screenshot of the young man with the new leather jacket in his hands and a scorpion tattoo on his neck.

***

"Here for a late lunch?" Eddie Ray asked when Lottie got back to the bar in Cloudcroft. "Got a bacon cheese-burger special going on today."

"Here for a bite of someone's ass." Lottie stalked by the smiling bar owner to the kitchen. Ricco Hernandez, the greasy dishwasher, was carrying a tray of glasses from the wash station when he looked up and spotted her holding the screenshot.

The tray slipped from his hands. Glass shattered. Still in his apron, he shot through the back door.

Lottie bolted after him, glass shards grinding under-neath her heels. Ricco hopped on a junker bike near the Dumpster on the far side of the parking lot. He jammed a key in the ignition and cranked. The engine coughed and sputtered then died. He swore. She swore louder as she hoofed it across the parking lot. Less twenty pounds and twenty years, she'd have his ass already pinned to the ground.

Again he crammed his boot heel into the starter. A belch of smoke defiled the air, and the bike roared to life.

She reached into her bag and pulled out her service revolver. Huffing way more than she should, she said, "You may be able to outrun my fat old ass, Ricco, but you can't outrun my Glock."

***

Ricco sat on a stack of boards near the Dumpster, toeing fine dust into a pile. "I swear, Sergeant King, I have no idea what happened to your friend. I found the wallet in the parking lot the night he stopped for dinner."

This kid was going from dumb to dumber. "I do believe your shift ended well before Gil James left. Kind of hard for him to pay for his dinner without a wallet." She aimed a finger, as hard and dark as the barrel of her Glock, at his forehead. "Talk."

He flinched, as if the single word were a bullet. At last he kicked at the dust pile. "I came back to the bar after hours to, uh, pick up something I left at work and spotted the wallet in the parking lot."

More like pilfer something from his boss, but she didn't have time for petty theft. "What time?"

"Around eleven. The wallet was just laying on the ground. No one around. I swear."

"You decided to take Mr. American Express on a little

shopping spree to El Paso that night?"

"Yeah. I thought I better use it before someone reported it missing."

So Ricco wasn't a total dumb shit. "And the man who owned the wallet, Gil James, where was he?"

"I told you, I found just the wallet. The guy and his bike were gone."

She needed to squeeze hard and see what came out of this grease ball. "I'm sure this isn't the first time those slick fingers of yours nicked something around here." Lottie crossed her arms over her puffed up chest. "Bet you skimmed stuff from Eddie Ray, a hard-working guy barely squeaking by."

Ricco squirmed.

"What I'm not sure about is what you did to Gil James."

"Not a thing. I swear on my life." Ricco leaned toward her, so close she could see the grease in his pores. "The wallet was already on the ground. I didn't do nothing to that guy."

Lottie carried a number of items in her bag. Unfortunately, a bullshit detector was not one of them. So right now she had to rely on her years of experience. Ricco was looking her in the eye. No blinks. No tiny balls of sweat. She'd bet her oldest grand's college fund that Ricco was telling the truth.

Chapter Three

Little Gil was right. Something was wrong. The rogue wallet was proof. A man did not part easily with his beloved AmEx.

A deputy with the Otero County Sheriff's office drove off with Ricco, and the sheriff officially started the manhunt for Gilbert James, Senior. Although the able-bodied locals were on the case, Lottie wasn't ready to hang up her stilettos. So far she'd tracked down everyone in the bar except Tolliver, the drug dealing scum. After phone calls to Tolliver's probation officer, neighbor, and ex-wife, Lottie finally tracked him to Silver Lake where he sat on the end of a dock, a fishing line and his feet dangling in the water.

She took a seat next to him and took out her shield.

He glanced at the bling then back at the lake. "I didn't do it."

Lottie looked in his tackle box. Feathered lures. Faded bobbers. Spearmint gum. A knife with a wicked curve on the end. "Little premature since I didn't ask a question yet."

"I haven't been in Colorado in thirty years, not since a family fishing trip to Groundhog Reservoir in the early eighties, so whatever you're investigating, it don't involve me."

She studied one of his boots. Big. "But Gil James might."

"Don't know any Gils. Don't know any Jameses. So go away, Colorado Cop Lady." He lifted his face to the cloudless sky. "It's seventy-five degrees, and the fish are biting."

"Gil James was at Eddie Ray's two nights ago. He rode in here on a vintage Harley. You see him?"

Tolliver shrugged. The jerky movement was meant to be casual, but he looked like he was stretching skin suddenly too tight. "Sure, I remember the guy and the bike."

"And?"

"And nothing. I left the place right after he arrived around nine thirty or so. Ask Sandy the bartender."

"Did you talk to Gil James?"

"Nope."

"You sure about that?" She pointed to his pole, bouncing compliments of his shaky hands. "You seem a little rattled."

Tolliver jerked the pole and reeled in the line. "I'm sure. He was talking to Marv and Millie from the gift shop. They saw me. Wave-wave. I didn't say a word to no one."

"And the bike? Did you check it out?"

"Nope." The line whirred faster, like an agitated bumble bee. "I got straight on my bike and took off."

"Where'd you go?"

"Home."

"Anyone there who can verify that?"

"My pet gold fish."

Lottie whipped out her phone. "I got your parole officer on speed dial, and if you don't tell me the truth, I'm calling and telling him you were involved in the assault and disappearance of Gilbert James, Senior."

Tolliver's knuckles whitened. "I did not hurt that man."

Lottie's nostrils flared. She could smell it, whiffs of fear with a hint of a man wanting to make a deal. "But you were there when something happened to him."

He said nothing, and she punched a button on her phone. She didn't have bars, but he was probably too stupid to notice.

"Okay, I was there," Tolliver said. "How'd you know?"

Lottie pointed at his boot. "Found some big boot prints near the wooden railing where Gil had his bike parked. Not too many size fourteens walking this earth." She pointed to the spearmint gum in the tackle box. "The green gum was the clincher. So talk."

Tolliver fiddled with a knob on his reel. "I didn't lie. I left Eddie Ray's at nine thirty."

"But you didn't go straight home." She was getting tired of reeling this guy in.

"I met with a buddy in the woods behind Eddie's place." A meeting that most likely involved an illegal substance or two.

"What time?"

"Must have been right after ten. From where I stood in the woods, I heard Sandy and your friend talking. Sandy got in her truck, and your friend hopped on his motorcycle. My guy still hadn't showed, so I walked down the road, thinking maybe I was in the wrong spot. My pal wasn't there. When I got back to my waiting spot, I checked to make sure your motorcycle guy was gone. At first I thought he was, but then I saw him lying on the ground, the bike on top of him."

A heavy breath settled in the center of her chest. "Was there anyone nearby? Any sounds?"

"No one, and I didn't hear any gunshots or fighting, if that's what you want to know."

"You just left a man there with a bike on top of him?"

"No, Sergeant King. I've done some questionable things in my lifetime, but I'm not big on people dying. I ran over to the parking lot and heaved the bike off him. There was a cut on his arm, but nothing major. No gushing blood. No crushed bones." Tolliver's fingers stilled on the reel. "But his chest wasn't moving. No air coming out of his nose or mouth. No pulse. I spit out my gum and tried mouth-to-mouth, but the guy was dead."

Lottie pulled in a fast breath, the rush of air pushing away the image of the victim. Cop now. Friend later. "And?"

"The guy I was meeting, he arrived. So I went and took care of some business. When I came back to call nine-one-one, your guy was gone, and I don't mean just dead. He'd disappeared."

"The bike?"

"Gone."

"Okay." The weight on her chest eased. "You were wrong about him not breathing. Gil was obviously still alive and took off on his bike."

"Not likely. A revving Harley is pretty hard to miss, and I swear, Sergeant King, your friend was dead."

No. She'd need to see that lifeless body with her own eyes before admitting that to herself or Little Gil. "What time did you get done with your business?"

"A little after ten thirty. I'm sure of it because Eddie Ray had turned off the bug zapper light and was gone for the night."

"Why should I believe a drug-dealing scumbag like you?"

He locked gazes with her. "I'm talking to you right now, Colorado Cop Lady. I'd rather get busted for dealing than murder."

***

Holding her phone in one hand, Lottie stood in the parking lot of the Cloud Top B&B where the cell coverage was good and aimed a shaky finger at the SEND button. Miss.

Gil James—the quiet, bookish boy at the back of the classroom, the sweet guy who bought her ice cream—was missing and according to a drug dealer named Tolliver, definitely dead.

Her quaking hand tightened around the phone. At last she managed to get the call through to the sheriff, telling him what Tolliver had seen during his drug deal.

"We'll bring Tolliver in, push some buttons, and see if we can get anything else out of him," the sheriff said. "I'll also get men and our SAR dog on the land behind Eddie Ray's."

Search and rescue dog. Not cadaver dog. Until they had proof otherwise, this was a search and rescue effort.

Before she put away her phone, she played her messages. Only one.

Beeeeep.

"Uh, hi, Sergeant King. This is me. Gilbert James. The Third. I know I only paid you for one day, but I'd like to keep you on the case. I washed my mom's car and earned some money. So, we're good for another day. Okay? Let me know if you need me to send you a picture of the ten dollar bill."

She texted: STILL ON THE CASE.

Back in town, Lottie pulled into Eddie Ray's, the parking lot empty but for two bikes. Behind the building, dust fanned up from dirt roads as the sheriff's people searched for Gil and a sweet bike with cherry red paint and gold flame striping. She ground a heel into the dirt. Everything kept coming back to the Harley, the bike that changed Old Gil's life. Did it somehow lead to his death?

Last night she learned on an Internet search that a similar bike went for almost one hundred thousand last year at auction. Was it possible someone killed Gil to get to that bike? Lottie leaned her butt against the hitching post. They were looking at a relatively small window of time for the Big Bad to do his deed. Sandy, the bartender, left the bar at ten with Gil. Tolliver, the drug-dealing scum, found Gil down around ten fifteen, but when he came back after ten thirty, Gil and the bike were gone. Eddie Ray, who closed up shop at ten thirty, concurred. So it had to be someone close by, someone who could move Gil and that bike. Someone with something that could haul.

The hair on the back of Lottie's neck stood on end as she pictured the bartender. Sandy was small but muscled, and she had a truck. As a bartender, she could have easily slipped something into Gil's drink to knock him out or even kill him.

Her heart rate ratcheting up a few notches, Lottie hurried around the side of the building where employees parked. There she found two trucks, including a smaller, older one with a green bandana hanging from the rear-view mirror. She leaned over the side and searched the truck bed. No blood. No red or gold paint.

She rubbed at the back of her neck. Was she getting desperate? Losing her edge? Was the kid getting to her? An old flame? Her hands plopped to her sides. Or maybe she was too old, too tired. It had been more than three months since she had a day off. As for vacation. *Pffffft*. It had been years since she had a vacation. She and her old friend Ruthie always planned to take a Caribbean cruise after they retired. Lottie's throat thickened. Ruthie was gone. As for Lottie? She had a killer to catch.

Spinning on her heels, she checked out the other truck, a shiny new four-by-four. On the lip of the tailgate she spotted red. Not a shiny paint chip. This was dark and dried, a bricky red. As in dried-blood red. Her toes twitched, and she climbed on the bumper.

The door opened behind her, light spilling out. "Hey, Sergeant King, what are you doing on my truck?"

Lottie spun to face Eddie Ray, the teddy bear bar owner. "Needed to get some elevation. Sheriff's guys are out in the woods looking for Gil James."

Eddie Ray wiped a dishtowel across his forehead. He was flushed and sweaty, probably from running the grill. Another guy chained to his job. "Still no word on your friend?"

"Nothing yet." She hopped down and ran her hand along the rim of the truck bed, stopping just shy of the bricky red. "She's a beauty."

"Thanks, bought her a few months ago."

"Four wheel drive is nice. Use it much for getting out in the woods, fishing or hunting?"

"Nope. I'm not into outdoor stuff. I'm more of a gear head."

Someone who liked cars and bikes. She made her way along the length of the truck. "I ran into Tolliver today. He was fishing. You're right; the guy's a real scumbag."

Eddie Ray tucked the towel into his waistband. "I'm telling you, if something happened to your pal, I bet you a night's worth of receipts, Tolliver had a hand in it."

"We found out Tolliver was here the night Gil disappeared." She pointed to the shadowy woods behind the building. "Out there doing a drug deal. You didn't by any chance see him or his drug buddy, did you?"

"No, but come to think of it, I did see some lights in that area when I left."

"Timing is important." She walked around to the other side of the truck, her gaze glued to the bed liner. "What time?"

"Like I told you, I left right at ten thirty."

"Good." Lottie nodded. Was that red paint on the wheel well? The twitch in her toes inched up her legs. "Which way did you exit the property?"

"Went out to the main road and turned right."

"You drove straight home?"

"Yep."

And there. That sure as hell was a sliver of gold. Her heart jolted. "Got home about what time?"

"Must have been ten forty-five or so. I live a few miles off the highway."

"Hmmmmm."

Eddie Ray turned back to the door. "Let me know if I can do anything, Sergeant King."

"Is there someone who can verify that you arrived home at ten forty-five?"

Eddie Ray turned slowly. "Why?"

"Just working the timeline, and I need confirmation on what time you got home."

"My wife was home."

Lottie nodded. "Can you give me her name and number? I need to make it all official, the timing thing, you know."

Eddie Ray's bulk shifted. "She was asleep." Another shift, like a big ol' bear with a thorn in his paw.

Good. Now for a poke to the bear's ass. "Eddie, where did you go after locking up your bar on Tuesday night?"

The bar owner paced like a bear in a circus cage. Trickles of sweat that had nothing to do with a hot grill ran down the sides of his face. "I was at a friend's house. A, uh, lady friend."

"And this lady friend?" Lottie asked. "She can vouch for you?"

"Yeah, but don't tell my wife, please." There was something angsty, almost desperate in his voice.

"Lady friend got a name? Contact information?" Because this guy also had dried blood in the back of his truck, not to mention something that looked like red and gold paint from a newly restored vintage Harley.

"Of course." Eddie slapped his shirt and apron pockets. "I'll have to get it later. I need to get back to the grill."

She reached into her bag and took out the Hello Kitty pen and pad. He hesitated before scrawling a barely legible name and address on the paper.

Yep, this guy was hiding something. "No phone number?"

"We don't do much talking." Eddie Ray winked and slipped into the restaurant.

She turned to her Jeep when she spotted two deputies poking through the woods about a hundred yards from the bar and grill, no doubt looking for Gil, and if she had her way, a very much *alive* Gil.

She hitched her bag on her shoulder and trekked through the brush to the tree line where she greeted a deputy with a nod. "Anything?"

"Not yet."

"Good. That's good." No dead body. When she found her old friend, she'd give him a hard time for putting them all through the wringer, particularly his grandson. Then she'd demand a ride on that old bike. Ice cream, too. "Listen, I need you to contact the sheriff and get a guy on the bar and stick him on Eddie Ray. If he goes anywhere, I want him followed."

"Eddie, the owner? He's a great guy. He had some tough breaks lately with the bad economy and slow ski season last winter, but he's hanging in there."

Eddie also had blood in the back of his truck. He wasn't a hunter. He was a gear head, a guy who loved cars and motorcycles. Did he love 'em enough to kill?

Chapter Four

According to Eddie Ray, his lady friend's name was Cindy, and she lived a mile past the Cloud Top B&B. The sun hadn't yet tucked in for the night, and a golden sky stretched above Lottie as she drove up and over the mountain. Even in the warm glow of day, the drop was sinister. Lance-like pines. Rocks as sharp as a saw blade.

As she drove down the first set of switchbacks just past the B&B, she breathed in the cool mountain air. Didn't help. Something hot and tingly pulsed through her body. She was getting close. She rounded the first hairpin turn. Something big and burly rushed across the road. She pictured bear-like Eddie Ray, but it was a white-tailed deer. She swallowed a laugh. Yep, that man was on her mind.

The road narrowed, and she took her foot off the gas. Up ahead she spotted a two-story cabin with a pointed blue roof. She itched to go faster, but she kept the car slow and steady. At the next switchback, she tapped the brake.

The Jeep didn't slow.

She pumped. Air whooshed.

The Jeep picked up speed.

She grabbed the emergency brake. Shit! Locked.

Rocks kicked up from her tires, plinking faster. Trees rushed by in a blur of gray-green.

She grabbed the gear shift and yanked. Didn't budge. She leaned into the shifter. The handle snapped and fell to the floor with a thud.

"Damn!"

The next switchback loomed ahead. She cranked the wheel, weaving long arcs across the road. The Jeep slowed, and she took the turn. Her outer wheels hit the soft shoulder. Rocks fell like silent rain into the abyss. She forced her gaze back on the road and jammed hard toward the rocky face. The car jolted as the tires found traction.

No time for a sigh of relief. She tackled the backside of the hairpin turn. Road narrowed. Jeep gained more speed. There was no way she'd make the next turn.

She yanked the steering wheel. Jammed the side of her Jeep into the rocky face. The metal frame split as if sliced by a can opener. Dust poured in and clawed up her throat, peppered her eyes, but she could still see the edge of nothing. She was headed straight for the cliff.

All grew silent. No whirring tires. No rush of wind.

And then came one voice. Not her three girls or seven grandchildren. Not a co-worker or one of her many mentors.

That bike changed him. Gave him the courage to leap.

Lottie wrenched open the door. A wave of piney dust slammed her. Far, far below, the earth spun.

She pulled in a breath and leaped.

For seconds, her body hung in midair.

The world slowed. The sun glinted off dust particles like slow-blinking Christmas lights. The wind rolled over her in sluggish waves. A bird called out, the cry low and rolling, like a gospel choir. The car, her ancient Jeep that creaked and groaned almost as much as her knees, crept to the edge of the road, peeked over, and dove into the abyss.

Wham!

She slammed into the washboard road. White-hot pain exploded across her shoulder. She curved into herself and rolled. Pin-sharp needles dug at her arms. Rocks gouged her back. She clawed at the earth. Clods of dirt and dried pine slipped through her fingers. She flexed her toes, fighting for traction and found air.

Air above. Air below.

Down, down she fell.

Her foot hit something hard. Her ankle bone cracked. She groaned.

Air rushed up her skirt, pulled at her hair. She grasped and clutched and finally wrapped her fingers around a pine sapling with the hand of her good arm.

For one crazy moment she thought of another sapling, a tiny peach tree she planted in her backyard forty-odd years ago, the one that hid a murder weapon. She'd come so far. So far since the days she'd buried that gun and walked the world in thrift store shoes and other people's sweat.

Her grip on the pine sapling tightened. She still had so much to do. More peaches to pick. New shoes to buy. Grandbabies to help win the Heisman.

If she was going down, she wasn't going easy.

She jammed the pointy toes of her stilettos into the side of the mountain, a lance of pain shooting through her ankle.

The pine sapling stretched. The earth groaned.

She held tight.

The sapling held firm.

Her heart hammering her chest, Lottie took stock. She was on a soft ledge covered with a sea of pine saplings about ten feet below the lip of the cliff. Below her... Nope. Not going there. She'd made the only leap she needed today.

Up. All she needed to do was go up, which meant grabbing onto one little sapling after another and moving toward the sky. The story of her life.

Identifying the fattest sapling, she reached, ignoring the sledgehammer pounding her shoulder and foot, and gave a gentle tug. The tiny tree held tight. Thank the Lord of all things great and small.

Leg up. Hand up. Don't look down.

This would be easier if she'd had the time to work out and eat right.

Leg up. Hand up. Don't look down.

Six feet from the top, she heard the happiest of sounds. The roar of an engine. A car door slamming.

"Down here," she cried. "Down here!" Leg up. Hand up. Don't look down.

Footsteps pounded above her. A hand reached for hers. She grabbed it, heaving herself forward and into the face of...

Her throat spasmed. "Eddie Ray."

"No," the bar owner said around a choked breath.

"This wasn't supposed to happen."

"Pull me up, Eddie, and we can talk."

His body didn't move, but the features of his face fell. She'd seen the look often in the assholes she'd booted into jail. Sadness. Regret. The guy—a self-professed gear head—must have done something to her car, most likely her brakes.

"Pull," she demanded.

Eddie Ray's head snapped as if slapped, and he pulled, but then he stopped, sadness giving way to fear. "No, I can't. You know too much."

"I know nothing, Eddie. I honestly don't know what the hell is going on." At least not the full story.

Eddie Ray wrenched his gaze from their clasped hands to her face. "I didn't kill your friend. I'm not a murder-er." He tugged at her fingers.

She gripped tighter. "I believe you." She swallowed the boulder in her throat. "Gil was already dead when you locked up and left the building."

Eddie Ray blinked. "You believe me?"

Guns were overrated in her business. Words were one hell of a weapon. "Absolutely. Tolliver can back you up. He was there. He tried to revive Gil."

Eddie Ray's head jerked in a fast series of nods. "Me, too. I did the chest thing and mouth-to-mouth thing, but he was gone. I swear, he was dead."

"So it's all okay. Help me up, and we'll talk to the sheriff together."

"No, it's not okay." He looked over his shoulder. "I took the bike. Already got a buyer for it. Seventy-thousand. That kind of money's gonna save my bar, my family's livelihood. Rough year. Another bar opened down the street. Winter ice-storm knocked down part of my roof. Had to lay off my line cook and two waitresses. I'm just a hard-working stiff trying to earn a living, trying to support a family."

"Exactly, Eddie Ray, but the minute you let go, you become a killer." The last word echoed in the canyon below. "If you let go, this moment will haunt you every day of your life. Every time you breathe in the scent of pine, every time your boots walk down a dirt road, you will remember this moment. You will remember that you are a cold-blooded murderer."

Eddie Ray closed his eyes. Was he praying for guidance? Letting her words soak in? Blocking out what he was about to do?

The tiny ledge below her right foot gave way. Rocks tumbled. Her other foot slipped. She grabbed another sapling, but it tore from the earth. She fell a foot, bringing Eddie Ray over the edge.

"Pull!" Lottie roared.

Something snapped in Eddie Ray. He blinked and shook his head, like a bear coming out of hibernation. He lunged back, and she jerked upward. She found another foothold.

He heaved. She pushed.

Finally, she landed on the road, her body pressed against the dirt in a passionate embrace.

Crawling to one hand and her knees, she cradled her bad arm and sat her ass on the road. There was no way her ankle would hold her. Only then did she look below at the one-hundred story drop. A spike of nausea rushed up her throat.

Eddie Ray continued to stare out at the canyon.

"Get back, Eddie Ray" she demanded.

He didn't move.

She reached for his calf.

He shrugged her off. Then he took a sweat-soaked towel from his waistband. Letting the towel fall to the ground, he leaped.

"Nooooo!" Lottie lunged for Eddie Ray but grabbed only air.

Chapter Five

Lottie hobbled to her front door, one foot wrapped in an Ace bandage, the other tucked in a butt-ugly white Ked. She opened the door and found Little Gil standing on the porch. This time she was the one with a tear-streaked face. After a few hours in the ER last night where the doc reset her shoulder and treated a severely sprained ankle, one of the Otero County deputies drove her home seeing as her old Jeep was in its final resting place at the bottom of a New Mexico canyon. She'd snagged a few hours of sleep and this morning woke up well enough for a good cry for Old Gil.

"Here." Little Gil opened his fingers. On his palm sat a crumpled ten dollar bill. "Granddaddy said a man always paid his debts."

Because Old Gil was a good man, and his grandson was following in his footsteps. A fine legacy for any soul.

"Thank you, Gil." She tucked the money into her sling and motioned to the porch step. "Everything okay?" She searched his face. No trembling lip today.

"Mom and Dad are pretty upset."

"You?"

"I knew Granddaddy was gone when he didn't call,

so I've had a few more days to deal with it."

Because a grandson knew these types of things. The search and rescue dog had spotted up on Gil's body yesterday evening off a forest road near Silver Lake.

"The funeral is on Tuesday," Gil said. "Dad wanted to make sure you knew, in case you wanted to come seeing as how you and Granddaddy were old friends."

Old Gil had very much been an old friend. He'd helped her with math, bought her ice cream, and could have been an old flame if she hadn't been too blinded by Charles.

"I'd like that very much."

Gil swiped his sneaker across the porch step. "We got the report back from the doctor. He said Granddaddy died of a heart attack, a massive one that took him right away."

"I'm sorry."

"Me too." Gil squared his shoulders. "I'm also sorry about Eddie Ray. That sucks."

The sheriff had called her this morning. Eddie Ray Walter's death had not been instant. A deputy had arrived just as Eddie leaped off the side of the mountain, and within an hour, the rescue team fished him out of the canyon. He'd broken his back, busted both legs, and crushed his ribcage. Internal bleeding finally did him in.

Eddie Ray started out as a hard-working guy just trying to make a living, but something had changed him. Was it not being able to support his family? The death of a dream? He'd saved her, but in the end he was indeed a killer.

"He was a sad man," Lottie simply said.

"But you know what, Sergeant King? Granddaddy was just the opposite. He died happy. I'm sure of it." Gil, who'd been looking at his sneakers, peeked at her with a smile. "Mr. American Express told me so."

"Really? This I gotta hear."

"According to the detailed report from the credit card, Granddaddy had pancakes and sausage for breakfast and a glass of orange juice, extra large. That was his favorite breakfast. Then he took off on his bike and rode through all those great mountains then stopped at Super Target. You know what he bought? A mystery book and a giant candy bar. One with nuts. Then he got to a little town in the clouds where he left a big tip for a waitress and ate apple pie. It was a good day, Sergeant King. He didn't die in a hospital hooked up to machines like Grandma. He died doing what he loved."

Lottie swallowed three times before she could speak. "You're a wise young man."

Gil nodded, his face so serious she almost laughed. He stood and wiped his hands on his jeans. "You're paid in full, so I guess we're done." He held out his hand. "Thank you, Sergeant King."

She shook. "Glad to be of service." As Gil ambled down the walkway, she called out, "Hey, did you ever find out what your granddaddy got you for your birthday?" According to Mr. American Express, Old Gil had spent more than three hundred bucks at a toy store last week.

"Not yet." A smile flitted onto the boy's mouth. "If I can't find it, maybe I'll hire you to investigate."

"Excellent because I have a special deal for my repeat

customers."

She sat on the porch watching until Gilbert James the Third was just a spec. Even then, she didn't move. Unfortunate as Scott Traynor, her partner, would be by in fifteen minutes to drive her to work. Important work. Work that involved catching killers, the best job in the world.

Down the street a group of kids rode bikes toward the park. She spotted little Jay-Jay with his football. A bit more practice and that boy would be a shoe-in for the Heisman.

She really did need to spend more time tossing the pigskin with him. With all the grands. And her three daughters. She had a fine family. The ache in her shoulder spread down to her chest and squeezed her heart. A family she would never have seen again in this world if things on that winding mountain road had ended differently. She readjusted her arm in the sling. Hell, her ticker could have clocked out like Gil's. Or like her old friend Ruthie, she could have been gunned down by a Big Bad with evil on his mind.

Old Gil. Ruthie. Two beautiful souls from her past. The ache clawed its way to her gut. But they weren't destined to be part of her future.

She pictured her old friends. Gil riding his Harley. Ruthie pouring coffee for a woman in need. They'd both died doing what they loved.

Lottie had the best job in the world, but she was tired and slowing down. She refused to look at that butt-ugly Ked. She still had plenty of good years in her, and although she loved catching killers, it was time to spend time with other things she loved: her girls, the grands, baking, shoe shopping, and maybe even that cruise.

It was time to pull a Gil and leap.

Buttermilk-Crusted Blackberry Cobbler

Best dessert ever. Seriously. Put down the book and go make this now.

Yield: Serves 8; Prep time: 20 minutes; Cook time: 1 hour; Total Time: 1 hour 20 minutes

Ingredients

Filling:

1-1/2 pounds fresh Marion blackberries (frozen triple berry mix is great, too)

1 cup sugar

3 1/2 tablespoons flour

1 tablespoon vanilla extract

Crust:

2 tablespoons sugar

1 1/2 teaspoons baking powder

1/2 teaspoon salt

2/3 cup butter

1 cup buttermilk

2 1/3 cups flour

Topping:

1 tablespoon melted butter

1 tablespoon sugar

Vanilla ice cream (optional)

Directions

1. Preheat oven to 350 degrees and grease a large casserole dish.

2. In a medium bowl, combine berries, sugar, flour, and vanilla. Pour into greased dish.

3. In a large bowl, mix sugar, baking powder, and salt. With a pastry cutter, cut in butter. Add buttermilk and 1 1/2 cups of flour to form a sticky dough. Spread remaining flour on work surface and knead dough until most of the flour is incorporated. Roll dough to 1/4-inch thickness and cut into 2-inch pieces. Cover berry filling with dough, overlapping pieces.

4. Drizzle melted butter over dough; sprinkle with sugar.

5. Bake at 350 degrees until crust is golden brown and filling is bubbly, about one hour. Cover with foil if getting too brown.

6. Serve warm over vanilla ice cream.

Author's Note: If you moved in next door to me, I'd make this recipe and deliver it to you with a hug and a smile. If you had a baby, got married, or lost a beloved, I'd make this for you. Blackberry cobbler is my go-to dish for potlucks, family get-togethers, and times when I need something sweet and good bubbling in my kitchen. I usually use heart-shaped cookie cutters for the dough because...well, that's how I roll. In my world the ice cream is not an option. Enjoy!

From the creative kitchen of award-winning author
Shelley Coriell
www.shelleycoriell.com

Smooth Sailing

A Detective Lottie King Mystery

Chapter One

Lottie's red peep-toed heels pounded the tile floor, the sound ricocheting like gunshots in the early-morning quiet of the second-floor offices of CSPD. "Where the hell is it?"

Her soon-to-be-former-partner, Colorado Springs homicide detective Scott Traynor, didn't lift his gaze or fingers from his computer. "Where's what?"

"The chocolate fountain."

"Why are we getting a chocolate fountain?"

"My retirement party."

Someone at the back of the room snorted. One bozo chuckled.

Her partner looked at her over the top of his monitor. "The day you retire, Sarge, is the day I grow alfalfa out my ass."

Lottie dug into the recycling bin and plucked out an empty box. "Well, get you some clippers, Mr. Master Gardener, because I am retiring. To. Day."

Traynor pushed back from his desk and crossed his arms over the holster holding his Sig P226. "And what are you going to do with yourself when you *retire*?"

Lottie'd been too busy wrapping up cases and

reassigning those still under investigation to make any immediate plans, but, frankly, she wasn't too worried about plans. "I'm going to put up my feet and relax."

The team in homicide erupted in laughter.

"No joke." She tossed the box on her desk. "At five p.m. sharp it's *bon voyage*."

"We've been down this road before," Traynor said. "You threatened to retire after you put the wrap on the Broadcaster Butcher case. You swore you were done, but when it came time to walk, you couldn't do it."

She rubbed the scarred flesh at her shoulder where this past summer the serial killer known as the Broadcaster Butcher had sunk his eight-inch double-edged knife. A few inches to the right, and her seven grandkids would have lost their batting coach, SAT tutor, and head cheerleader. The truth was, the whispers of her retirement—both in the office and in her head—had started long before that nasty business with the Butcher. For more than three decades Lottie had served and protected, and she'd collared a hell of a lot of Big Bads, but over the past few years, she'd lost a bit of speed and gained a few pounds. For some time now, her head and body had been urging her to call it quits. Her heart had been the lone holdout.

Last month that big, booming muscle in the center of her chest finally got the memo when an old friend died of a heart attack while taking a road trip on his beloved vintage Harley. A twinge stole across her chest. A sad moment for sure, but her old high school friend's death opened her eyes. So had hanging off the side of a cliff just days after her friend's heart attack. When she was staring death in the face, she didn't want to die surrounded by

Big Bads. Nope. She wanted her girls and the grands. Of course, that was after a few good shoe shopping trips and a Caribbean cruise or two.

With a snap of her wrist, Lottie grabbed a photo from her desk. "This time I mean it. I'm retiring." She packed the photo of her six-year-old granddaughter at her kindergarten graduation in the box. "Enrique got a champagne fountain at his retirement party last year, but I want chocolate."

Her partner humored her with a smile. "Whatever you say, Sarge."

She'd added a dozen other photos to the box when Sergeant Tam walked into the room with a paper in his fist. "Drowning up at Stone Manor Heights. Drunk homeowner fell into his koi pond last night." He waved the paper at Jonah Bradley, the team's shiniest and newest homicide detective. "I want you on it, Bradley, from start to finish."

The nube hopped up from his desk so fast, his chair tipped and clattered to the floor.

This time Lottie joined in the round of chuckling. Gotta love the kid, so green and gung ho. It had been decades since she'd been a baby homicide detective, but she'd never forget her first criminal homicide case: Walter Ong, the seventy-seven-year-old owner of a convenience store gunned down by a tweaker for twenty-three bucks and seven cents. On that first case she'd had gushers of adrenaline shooting through her veins and unrelenting voices ricocheting through her skull.

Serve justice.
Find the truth.

Speak for the dead.

Within two days she'd found the scumbag meth-head and his smoking gun. Every Christmas since then, Lottie donated twenty-three dollars and seven cents to a charity in Walter Ong's name. As long as she was alive, Walter Ong would continue to be heard.

Take that, Big Bads!

As Lottie started on the next drawer, footsteps pounded in the hallway. A voice shouted. Another. Every eye in the squad room, including hers, turned to the doorway where Lieutenant Rick Medina skidded to a stop, his face flushed.

"Big dust up at the Mountain Point Bank off Boulder," the lieutenant said. "Attempted robbery. Multiple gunmen. Hostages taken. Traynor, get your men over there. Now."

Lottie slammed the drawer. She reached for her service revolver at her hip but found only flesh. Panic nipped at her waist until she remembered she'd tucked her Glock in the locked bottom drawer of her desk. She was on desk-duty today, packing up and signing forms.

All around her, the team moved in swift synchronization. Guns in place. Phones at the ready. Game faces on. She studied her boys. A few stone-cold faces. Others laser-beam hot and sharp. More than one edged with a healthy dose of fear. Traynor's boyish, freckled nose scrunched in thoughtful concentration. Good. Her partner, an outstanding detective she'd trained, was already on the job and making plans to stop the Big Bads.

The lieutenant placed both hands on the edge of her packing box. "I'd be lying if I said we couldn't use you on something like this, Lottie. You're one of my finest."

Her toes, encased today in celebration-red shoes, twitched. Hell, yeah, she'd love to dive into this one, but she was headed to different waters. "Thank you, sir, but I'm done."

With a reluctant nod, he followed the team as they bolted out the door. Shiny shoes clacking. Jackets rustling. Steady murmur of voices. Someone in the office next door switched on a television. Outside sirens blared and helicopter blades spun.

Then came the quiet, creeping like an icy fog across her desk and into her bones. She could almost hear the gooseflesh popping up on the back of her neck, the blood in her veins slowing.

Oh God, is this what retirement sounds like?

Someone behind her cleared his throat. She spun and found Bradley, the nube homicide detective, looking at her with wide, worried eyes.

"You okay, Sergeant King?"

Lottie rubbed the tops of her arms, warming the chilled flesh. "Of course I'm okay," she said with a snap. Then she turned on a television on the back wall and scrolled through channels until she landed on a local news station broadcasting live from the skies above the Mountain Point Bank.

"A witness who'd been in the bank at the time of the robbery reported at least three armed men," the broadcaster in the passenger seat of a helicopter said over the *rota-rota-swoosh* of the chopper blades. "To date there has been one injury, but that could rise as the gunmen have taken seven hostages."

Seven hostages didn't mean seven deaths, Lottie reminded herself. Her boys were on the way, and while their job was to catch killers, the first job was to preserve life.

"I guess I need to leave now." Bradley's voice, just inches from her, made her jump. "I have the dead guy in the koi pond. I didn't hear the lieutenant say anything about me not going, did you? I should still go there, right?"

"Absolutely." She lowered the volume on the TV. "The first few days in any homicide are crucial, and the whopping majority of every case you ever handle will be solved within that forty-eight hour window."

He nodded, his lips pressed tightly and jaw working as if he were ingesting her words.

She wagged a hand in his face. "Now would be good time."

His jaw stilled. "I guess I'll see you around."

"At the retirement party tonight." She sat at her desk, flung open the next desk drawer, and found a tube of sunscreen. She checked the television, which now showed police units arriving. Had Traynor run out of the tube of sunscreen she gave him last month? That pale, freckled skin of his pinked up with just a few minutes of sun. Maybe she should take it to him.

Nope. She was retiring. To. Day. She tossed the tube on her partner's desk.

In the corner, Bradley rummaged through his desk and muttered words she couldn't hear.

"You okay?" Lottie asked.

"My phone." He slammed one drawer and opened

another. "I can't find it."

She watched him fumble and bumble for another full minute before she pointed to the clip on his belt. "Already locked and loaded."

His chin smacked his chest.

She bit back a smile. The kid was nervous, and he sure as shit should be. Bradley was going to pen the final chapter of a man's life today, and with that came great responsibility. The good thing was, the pup seemed to realize that already. "Jonah, you'll do fine."

He rolled his head along his shoulders before resting a gaze on the television that now showed officers suited up in SWAT gear. "I just want to do it right because..."

The TV camera zoomed in on a bloodstain near the ATM. "...because there's so much bad shit in this world," Lottie finished for him.

He nodded, his gaze pinned on the television screen.

She stood, the old chair creaking and groaning. Or maybe that was her body. Yep, she was getting old, but she had on a new pair of shoes. She liked the idea of showing them off. She grabbed the holster from her bottom drawer. "Come on, Guppy. Time to head to the koi pond."

"You're coming with me."

"Yep, but I'm stopping at five sharp."

A half smile curved the side of his mouth. "Okay."

"I'm not doing no paperwork. That's your job."

"Okay."

She thwacked him on the chest. "For Pete's sake, stop smiling." She snapped her holster in place, her Glock settling like a long-time lover's hand on her hip. "Doesn't look right to have a homicide detective grinning so damn much when he's going to check out a dead body."

Chapter Two

Detective Bradley let out a long, low whistle as they walked up the drive to a mansion where a man drowned in his koi pond. "Our Boy liked his toys."

Lottie squinted at the sleek black car. "How much does something like this shiny pony cost?" Last month she'd lost her crippled old Jeep Cherokee when it went over a cliff while she'd been tracking down a murder suspect in the mountains of New Mexico. She had a few pennies saved and wanted something sharp and snappy to wheel around in after she retired.

"Ferraris like this run about a quarter million."

She snorted. "For that kind of money, I could put two grands through college. What a waste."

Bradley motioned to the car's front tire, which was perched on the bricks of a flowerbed, the nose a half-inch from the garage door. "Looks like the driver was pretty wasted when he parked this thing."

The responding officer led them through the house. "The victim is Mitch Kesslar, forty-five-year-old male and the owner of this house. The wife found him this morning when she came home from visiting a relative in Denver. She and the next-door neighbor, a doctor, fished him out of the koi pond. They're both waiting in the kitchen to talk to you."

Bradley turned to follow the uni, but Lottie pulled him toward the back patio. "First, let's see what the body has to say."

Outside, the koi pond was sandwiched between a sandstone patio and putting green.

"According to the wife," the uni said, "Kesslar's company inked a major deal yesterday, and he celebrated after work with one too many glasses of champagne. When he arrived home he decided he needed a bit more celebrating." He pointed to a bottle of Gran Patron Platinum sitting on the patio bar next to an empty highball glass.

Lottie followed Bradley as he walked along the fishpond where water trickled over chunks of blue-gold granite and into a pool of water with wide-eyed orange fish swimming under crushed lily pads. They paused at the body sprawled on the pavers. Mitch Kesslar was a big man, one who clearly enjoyed his groceries. A raspberry bloomed on the side of his head. "Okay," she said. "Your turn. What do we *really* have?"

Bradley didn't hesitate. "This was no accident. Mitch Kesslar was murdered."

Excellent. Her fine city just might survive her retirement. "You know that because?"

"The wound on the head didn't come from a fall on those granite rocks. Too clean and symmetrical."

"As if made by..." Lottie prompted.

Bradley did that contemplative thing with his jaw again. "As if made by," he turned to the bottle of Patron, "a really nice bottle of tequila."

**

The examiner from the coroner's office placed the caliper against the wound on Mitch Kesslar's temple. "Perfect match. Blunt force trauma at the right temple matches base dimensions of the tequila bottle. Dark coloring of contusion indicates the blow occurred antemortem."

Lottie nodded. Confirmed. The victim was clubbed upside the head with a very expensive bottle of agave juice then fell or was pushed into the pond and drowned.

"Time of death?" Bradley asked.

"Ten twenty-one last night." The deputy coroner pointed to the guy's wristwatch. "His Patek Philippe broke when he fell into the pond."

At the patio table, Mr. Metro Crime Lab was lifting latent prints off the tequila bottle. "By the shape and size, it's clear we have two distinct sets," he said. "But even more significant, we found trace elements of blood on the base. This here's your murder weapon."

Bradley stared at the elegant silver and glass bottle with a thick, chunky base, his lips turning down.

"Do it," Lottie said. "Visualize glass slamming into his skull. Listen to the pop and crack of flesh and bone. Smell the blood and booze. Feel the pain of blunt force trauma to the brain."

Bradley breathed deeply.

"Got all that?"

He nodded.

"Don't ever forget it. Those are the final moments of the man you are putting to rest."

***

In the kitchen they found a slim, middle-aged blonde in a cream pantsuit sitting at a dining table and swirling a spoon in a porcelain teacup. The cup was empty.

Next to the woman sat a gray-haired man wearing scrubs and a pinched face. The man introduced himself as the Kesslar's neighbor, Dr. Niles Shaw. "I have to get to the hospital, so make this quick." He pulled a phone from the breast pocket of his scrubs, called up a call log, and thrust it in Bradley's face. "Melanie called me at eight-oh-two this morning, hysterical. She said Mitch fell into the fish pond and wasn't moving. I rushed over, and together we pulled him out. No respiratory activity or pulse. Flesh on appendages had already started to disassemble, and rigor had set in. Now if you'll excuse me, I have a surgery at ten, and I'd like to save at least one life today."

The doctor made to push past Bradley, but the new detective held his ground. "I need your cell and work number, sir, along with your work schedule today."

Good, the kid was being thorough and not letting the pompous doctor rattle him.

Now for Melanie Kesslar, the grieving widow whose face was the color and texture of the cream in the small pitcher on the tea tray. Her spoon continued to stir air.

Bradley cleared his throat. "Mrs. Kesslar?"

She didn't move.

"Mrs. Kesslar, would you mind?" Bradley motioned to the teapot sitting in the center of the table.

The woman blinked. "Excuse me?"

"It's early, and I didn't get a chance to stop for coffee." Bradley gave a sheepish grin. "Do you mind?"

"Oh, of course." Mrs. Kesslar busied herself with pouring tea, her movements smooth and practiced as she handed them both cups of steamy liquid. She even poured herself a cup. Good. The nube had pulled this woman out of her aching heart. Now time to get into her head.

Bradley took his time adding honey and cream to his cup. "What time did you arrive home this morning?" he finally asked.

Mrs. Kesslar lifted her spoon. *Tap. Tap. Tap.* "My plane from Denver landed at seven, and I arrived home around eight."

"Why were you in Denver?" Bradley asked.

"My mother had a stroke earlier in the week, a mild one, but I still wanted to be with her." Her bottom lip quivered, but she hid it with a long draw from the teacup. "Family is everything."

"You have children, right?" Bradley continued. "Were either of them in the house last night or this morning?"

"Alicia is away at college at Stanford. She's flying in this afternoon. She's a senior this year." Her lip trembled. "Mitch won't get to see her graduate." The woman's fingers tightened around the cup. "Our son, Andrew, lives here in Colorado Springs, but he has his own place near the Broadmoor."

"When you got home this morning, were there any signs of foul play? Anything missing or out of place?"

"Are you thinking Mitch's death wasn't an accident?"

For the first time, Bradley looked at Lottie.

Bradley was doing the dance, and it was time for her to take the lead and be the bearer of bad news. "I'm sorry to tell you, Mrs. Kesslar," Lottie said, "but your husband was murdered."

"Murder. Oh, God." Her voice rose in pitch and volume. "Who would want to kill Mitch?"

"That's why we're here, Mrs. Kesslar," Lottie said, keeping her words low and steady.

Bradley waltzed back in. "Did you find anything unusual when you got home?"

"The front door was unlocked, but that wasn't unusual given the way Mitch's car was parked. I figured he had a little too much to drink. He, uh, did that sometimes."

Lottie didn't like to talk ill of the dead, but dumbshits who drank and drove would not be receiving any Christmas cards from her.

"When was the last time you talked to your husband?" Bradley asked.

"Last night. He called to tell me the Aspen deal he'd been working on all year went through. His company designs and builds golf courses, and he'd poured a good deal of time and energy into getting the Aspen contract. It wasn't the biggest deal he'd ever made but one of the toughest. Mitch was over-the-moon thrilled. Said we were heading to St. Croix to celebrate."

"Does your husband have any enemies?"

"Everyone adored Mitch, his partner, employees, clients, people at the club. My husband was one of those people who didn't know a stranger."

"What about competitors? If he won the Aspen deal,

someone had to lose."

"I'm sure that's the case. His partner, Derrick Kemp, could tell you more."

"And in his personal life? Friends, neighbors, old school chums? Any arguments or altercations?"

Mrs. Kesslar shook her head. "Mitch is great with people, even uptight ones like Niles."

"Your neighbor, the doctor?"

"When we first moved in five years ago, there was a bit of tension," Mrs. Kesslar explained. "Mitch loved parties, and we did quite a bit of entertaining. Niles would complain about everything: noise, cars blocking his driveway, twinkle lights on the porch. He even started a neighborhood petition against Mitch. But Mitch, being Mitch, worked his magic. He made a sizeable donation to a children's charity Niles had started. Now Niles adores him." The soft smile on her lips wavered. "Or did."

"Are you telling me your husband never had words with anyone?" Bradley asked.

Mrs. Kesslar set down her cup, a trickle of thin liquid splashing over the rim and slithering over the glass tabletop like an anemic snake. "No. Never."

"Are you sure?"

Mrs. Kesslar jabbed a napkin at the spill.

"Mrs. Kesslar?" Lottie pressed.

The napkin fell into her lap. "Earlier in the week Mitch and Andrew had a tiny disagreement."

"Andrew is your son?" Bradley asked.

Mrs. Kesslar nodded. "It was nothing serious. Andrew joined the company in May and was getting up to speed, and Mitch felt he needed to go a little faster. They had a few words."

"A few?"

"Okay, more than a few. Andrew said he needed a salary increase, but Mitch said he had to prove himself first. It got so loud, Niles called the police."

More than a few words indeed.

After Bradley wrapped up his questions, Mrs. Kesslar escorted them through the house where they passed a baby grand piano and some fancy looking vases and sculptures.

"Mrs. Kesslar, upon your husband's death, who inherits his assets?" Lottie asked.

"Most of it goes to me. The business. The cars. The vacation homes in Sedona and Puerto Peñasco." A look of pure disgust washed over her face. "It's all for me." Then the dam broke. Tears fell. "I'd give it all away if I could have Mitch alive."

"You said *most* of the assets go to you." Lottie pushed through the woman's tears. Harsh, but necessary. "But not all?"

"Mitch has money earmarked for some valued employees and a few charities like the one Niles runs, and our children are sole beneficiaries of Mitch's life insurance policy."

"And the amount of that policy?" Bradley asked.

"Two million dollars."

Lottie's gut tightened. She'd seen people kill for less. Like twenty-three dollars and seven cents.

***

Bradley jammed his keys at the ignition but missed. Two more tries. Two more misses. The kid started fiddling with the keys.

Lottie kept silent. A good detective had an arsenal of questions, but a great one knew when to shut up.

"My wife and I just had our first kid," Bradley finally said. "A little boy. Four months old. Perfect little feet. Perfect little hands. He's just starting to smile. I swear, Sergeant, my son's smile brings me to my knees."

"And the idea that Mitch Kesslar's son, technically any son, could off his pop slams your gut."

"Like a cannonball."

"Here's the thing you gotta remember, Bradley. Ninety-nine percent of this world is good, but in homicide we spend most of our time with the one percent of bad, the maggots who don't respect life or themselves. Some detectives never get used to that one percent. It eats at their innards, and they beg to be transferred to property crimes. Those of us with the calling learn to stomach the Big Bads." She reached into her bag and unfastened a tiny zipper on one of the side panels. Inside was a small yellow sticky note, the stick having rubbed off ten or fifteen years ago. She set the paper on the dash. "For you, a little first-day-on-the-job present."

Bradley traced the two numbers written in pencil. "Ninety-nine." He breathed deeply, his lungs expanding and stretching his blazer. "Ninety-nine percent are good." He got the keys in the ignition, and they drove to the luxury condo complex where Andrew Kesslar lived. A bright red, two-door Mercedes sat in the driveway of Kesslar's condo.

Lottie ran her hand along the fancy car. "Like father, like son."

"But this one's for sale." Bradley pointed to the red sign in the back window. "You interested?"

She squinted at the asking price and snorted. "I could buy sixty pairs of Louboutins—with crystals—for that kind of money."

Bradley tapped on the door of Andrew Kesslar's condo. No answer.

Lottie cocked her head. *Swooooosh. Pop. Swooooosh. Pop.*

Around the side of the condo, she found a young man in low-riding basketball shorts and bare feet, hacking golf balls into a net.

"Mr. Kesslar? Andrew Kesslar?" Bradley said.

The young man gave them the hand. He squared up in front of the tee and drew the club back. *Swooooosh. Piffle.* The golf ball dribbled three inches from the tee.

Bradley flashed his shield. "We're here about your father. We're sorry—"

"Save it." Andrew Kesslar swung at another ball. A chunk of grass and the ball sliced to the right. "Mom told me. Someone gorked him. What do you need from me?"

Bradley's jaw tightened, and she caught his eye, warning him without words to tread lightly. Folks handled grief in many ways. Some bawled until their eyes swelled shut. Others talked to God. Still others acted like angry asshats.

Bradley cleared his throat. "When was the last time you saw your father?"

The son abused five more balls. "About six last night,

and he was very much alive and ripping me a good one at work."

"You and your father had words in the office last night?"

"Technically, we were in the parking lot. I called him a fat, greedy old turd and threatened to flush him down a stinkin' sewer where he belonged."

"What were you fighting about?"

The cocky kid's eyebrows knitted. "Do I need a lawyer?"

"I don't know, Mr. Kesslar, do you?"

The younger Kesslar gave an insouciant shrug and rested the golf club on his shoulder. "I asked him to front me a few bucks because I got behind on a few credit card bills. He told me no. I called him a tight ass, and he called me a waste of good semen. He told me to go home, sober up, and not to come to the office until I grew a few brain cells to go with my oversized balls."

"What did you tell him?"

"To go to hell." The son's voice broke, and for the first time, she saw a fissure in the anger and spotted the sadness below. "Then he walked away."

Lottie could barely make out that last word. "What did you do then?"

Kesslar re-gripped the club and took a swing at the ball. "I went to El Matador, a bar near the office, where I tossed back a few Coronas and picked up a beautiful girl named Tina." He scratched his left temple with the head of the golf club. "Or maybe it was Lena or Beana."

"And then?"

"We went to Tina/Lena/Beana's house and screwed

like rabbits until seven this morning when she had to leave for work." He waggled his eyebrows. "Would you like details?"

Bradley kept his cool. "I'll pass. Can she verify that you were at her place between ten and ten-thirty?"

"I'm pretty unforgettable."

"I'll need her name and contact information."

Kesslar held up his hand again, displaying a smudgy name and number, and smiled.

Back in the car, Bradley jammed the keys in on the first try. "Did you ever get the urge to hit a person of interest?"

"Yep. And there were a few I wanted to boot in the ass." Lottie clicked her seat belt. "Do you think Andrew Kesslar's telling the truth?"

Bradley frowned. "Not sure."

"What does your gut tell you?"

His frown deepened. "That Andrew Kesslar is an angry, screwed-up young man in a financial crisis, but he would never kill his father because he idolizes him too much. Hell, it's obvious the kid wants to be him."

Lottie patted his head. "You must have been a star pupil in Homicide School."

***

Mitch Kesslar and his partner, Derrick Kemp, owned K-2 Enterprises, a construction and property management firm that specialized in the design, building, and maintenance of high-end golf courses around the world.

"Pull in there." Lottie pointed to the covered parking

space reserved for Mitch Kesslar. "Because today *you* are his voice."

As they got out of the car, a white scooter puttered into the covered space marked for Derrick Kemp.

"Mr. Kemp?" Bradley called out.

The scooter driver, outfitted in proper safety gear—gloves, helmet, leather jacket—snapped off the helmet and nodded. He was thin and pale, as if he didn't get outdoors much, and wore khakis and wire-rimmed glasses, rocking the college professor look.

"We'd like to talk to you about Mitch Kesslar," Bradley said.

"Melanie called me this morning." Kemp pulled off his gloves and jammed them in his coat pocket. "Do you mind if we talk out here? I haven't told the staff yet." He ran both hands through his already rumpled hair. "It's going to be a rough day. Everyone loved Mitch, from the senior managers to the janitor. Mitch was the people guy."

"Which makes you?"

"The numbers guy. I take care of finances."

"You were partners?"

"Fifty-fifty. We've been working together for the past twenty-five years." Kemp's hands plopped to his sides. "I have no idea what we'll do now. I may have been the brains, but Mitch was the heart and lifeblood of the company."

"What's the status of the company?" Bradley asked.

"We've had record earnings for the past five years. We're in great shape."

"Last night you and Mr. Kesslar inked a deal for a golf

resort in Aspen?"

"Yes. Mitch had been working it for almost a year." Kemp's face paled. "I don't even know if we'll be able to keep the deal with Mitch gone."

"Anyone else vying for the contract?" Bradley asked.

"It came down to us and Pinnacle, a company here in the Springs. The owner's Jessie Navarro, our former marketing manager." Kemp's forehead wrinkled. "You don't think Pinnacle had anything to do with Mitch's murder, do you?"

"Do you?"

"I...I don't know. This is a tough business, and Navarro hasn't won a contract in the past year. But murder? That's...that's crazy."

Welcome to the wonderful world of homicide.

"When was the last time you saw Mr. Kesslar?" Bradley continued.

"I left the office around seven thirty, and he was still here."

"Was anyone else in the office?"

"Just me and Mitch. Everyone had cleared out by then."

"Did he seem nervous or upset?"

The corners of Kemp's mouth lifted. "At that point Mitch wasn't feeling much of anything. He'd had quite a bit to drink. I offered to drive him home, but he said he was expecting someone."

"Someone?" Lottie and Bradley said in unison.

"He didn't say who, just that someone was stopping by the office."

"Then you left?"

"No, then I took the keys to Mitch's Ferrari and ordered him a cab. He was way too drunk to drive, and I cared about him and this company enough to keep him off the roads."

Lottie pictured that catawampus Ferrari. "He must have skipped the cab. The car's at his house."

"Mitch took the cab home. I'm sure of it. I got an e-mail receipt at eight indicating Mitch had been delivered home." Kemp reached into his pocket. "Here are the Ferrari keys."

Which meant *someone* used another set of keys to get the Ferrari to Kesslar's fancy home in the Heights.

"For the record, Mr. Kemp, can you tell me where you were between ten and ten-thirty last night?"

"At home. Thursday's poker night. I've been playing with the same five guys for almost five years."

"They can vouch for you?"

"Yep, especially Frankie. I lost my shorts to him last night."

Chapter Three

Bradley handed her two ninety-nine cent street tacos, the waxy paper crackling where it wasn't soaked with grease.

She pasted on a mock scowl. "I knew I should have hung out with Traynor today. When he takes me to lunch, I get to use silverware." She took off the wrapper and drew in a deep breath of steamy, spicy air. She'd spent plenty of years eating ninety-nine cent tacos and two-for-a-buck corn dogs. She raised the taco in a salute to Bradley, but he didn't see. All he saw was the case. Good. She took a bite, savoring the chunks of onions, peppers, and machaca.

Bradley stared at his tacos, the grease spots growing.

"What's on your mind?" Lottie asked after another glorious bite.

"The Ferrari." Bradley picked up both tacos. "If Kesslar took a taxi home"—he parked a taco next to his soda—"how did the Ferrari get from the office to Kesslar's home?"

She took the second taco from his hand, made a few dips and turns, and placed it on its side next to the other taco. "Someone drove it."

"And because of the jacked-up parking job, it was someone who was drunk."

"Or possibly someone who simply wasn't used to that many horses under the hood."

Bradley picked up the taxi taco and downed it in four bites. "Or maybe Kemp is lying about the taxi. Maybe Mitch Kesslar wasn't waiting for *someone*. Maybe Kemp told us that because he killed his partner and wanted to throw us off track."

"Wouldn't be the first time."

Bradley downed the Ferrari taco. Three bites. "Why would he kill his partner? Losing Mitch Kesslar is bad for business. Both Kemp and Kesslar's wife said so. Plus Kemp alibis out."

Lottie polished off her taco and passed the second to Bradley. At her age, too much machaca past the lips meant beefy hips. Plus, she promised her middle daughter she'd start eating better once she was retired.

"So run with it," Lottie said. "Assume the partner is telling the truth and that Mitch Kesslar was meeting *someone*. How are you going to find out who?"

"Security cameras at the office could show a car or a person. I'll check with the K-2 office?"

"Good. What else?"

"The victim's appointment calendar could tell us if he was meeting someone, but that would be stupid, to schedule an appointment with Kesslar after hours then kill him." Two bites, and the third taco was history. This kid was working hard, burning serious calories.

"You have no idea what kind of stupid you're going to meet in this job," Lottie said. "The calendar's worth checking out."

"And his phone. I'd like to get a list of people Mitch Kesslar talked to that evening."

Lottie checked her watch. "The chocolate fountain for my retirement party is probably heating up, but we still got a few hours. Where to now?"

He gathered all of the taco wrappers and tossed them in the trash. Hard working and fastidious, too. Young Bradley could shape up to be one of CSPD's finest. "Back to the station. I need to make some calls."

Thanks to the on-going incident at Mountain Point Bank, the second floor was eerily silent. She checked in with the lieutenant's assistant. The seven hostages were still being held at gunpoint, but her colleagues had snagged one of the gunmen guarding the back entrance. She had no doubt her boys were gonna shut this down.

Bradley parked himself behind his computer, another powerful weapon in a detective's arsenal. She took a quick stroll down the hall and peeked into the conference room. No chocolate fountain. Yet. She sniffed. Someone had recently mopped the floor with pine cleaner. The coffee counter had been wiped down, the cups aligned in neat rows.

She grinned. Party central was spit-shined and lookin' fine.

Back in the squad room, she sat next to Bradley and settled her feet on a nearby desk. The red peep-toes were fun and festive, perfect for a party. Plus, she could dance in them in case there was music. Old Enrique had mariachi music at his retirement party. She could go for some good jazz.

Bradley tapped his computer screen. "Got Kesslar's call log. The last person he talked to was his wife. They had a seven-minute conversation at eight fifteen."

Lottie dragged her feet off the desk and rolled her chair so she sat shoulder-to-shoulder with Bradley.

"Prior to that, he made six calls to his son, Andrew."

"Could be the older Kesslar felt bad about calling his son a waste of good semen and wanted to apologize, or maybe he wanted to continue the fight. Either way, you need to check out that boy's voice mail. Could be interesting."

"As interesting as the incoming call at six-seventeen?" Bradley's eyes sparked. "The one from Jessie Navarro of Pinnacle, the owner of the company that lost out on the Aspen deal."

"Navarro could have called Kesslar to congratulate him."

"Or Navarro could have called to say, 'Hey, where are you going to be at ten twenty-one tonight so I can smash your skull with an expensive bottle of tequila?'" Bradley stood. "Either way, it sounds like a good time to visit this Jessie Navarro."

A good homicide detective was curious about his world and human nature. She was liking junior, here, more and more.

On the way to Navarro's office, Bradley's phone buzzed with a call from one of the Metro Crime Lab techs.

"Hey, Jimbo, what's up?" Bradley asked.

"Got hits on the prints on the tequila bottle. As expected, one set belongs to the victim. The other belongs to someone named Jessie Navarro."

How serendipitous. The same person they were on their way to see.

"Why's he in the system?" Lottie asked. Were they going to visit a suspect who'd already tangled with the law?

"Navarro did some government contract work a few years ago, so just a basic clearance-check, but, there is more to this story. We also found Navarro's prints on the Ferrari's steering wheel."

***

The reception desk of Pinnacle was a gray metal jobber with dents on the side panel, a far cry from the cherry wood and marble altar in the K-2 office. A secretary-type led them down a corridor with carpet snags and bad lighting and into an office with a view of the parking lot. Behind the desk sat a woman with bright red hair and nail lacquer to match, the only spot of color in the drab office.

"Jessie Navarro?" Bradley asked.

"And you would be?"

"Jonah Bradley and Lottie King of Colorado Springs PD. We need to talk to you about Mitch Kesslar."

A slow grin slid over her lips, also fire-engine red. "Did Midas Mitch finally make a mistake?" She waggled her fingers. "I can't wait to hear this one."

"Midas?"

"You know, everything Mitch Kesslar touches turns to gold. It gets a bit disheartening for those of us in competition with him."

"Last night Mitch was murdered."

The fiery woman's eyes widened, and her jaw tightened, sending spasms along her neck. "What happened?"

"Someone slammed a bottle of Gran Patron Platinum into his head and knocked him in a koi pond where he drowned."

Color drained from the woman's face, and Lottie knew it wasn't because of the loss of a two-hundred dollar bottle of booze.

"Just like the one over there." Lottie pointed to the bar in the corner of the room where a half dozen bottles of fine tequila sat. Jessie Navarro was a regular little connoisseur of agave juice.

Bradley spun. He'd been too busy studying Jessie Navarro, that he hadn't taken stock of the room. Lottie would have to talk to him about that.

The suspect shook her head. "No! I had nothing to do with Mitch's murder."

"Then why were your fingerprints on the bottle of tequila that killed him?"

She crossed her arms over her chest. "Because I gave it to him."

"You always send expensive gifts to competitors who take bread and butter from your own dining table?" Lottie asked.

"Mitch deserved this one. He worked his ass off and outsmarted me."

"Can you tell us why your fingerprints were on the steering wheel of Kesslar's Ferrari?"

"I drove it to his house," Navarro said as if she were saying the sky is blue.

"Why would you do that?" Bradley asked.

"Because he was drunk as a skunk and took a taxi before I got there."

"How'd you get the key?"

"Mitch gave it to me."

"Why?"

Jessie Navarro fiddled with the dozen gold bracelets on her wrist. *Clink. Clink.* The sound of puzzle pieces falling in place.

"Ms. Navarro?" Bradley prompted.

Jessie Navarro picked up the phone and punched the intercom button. "At this point I'd like to have my attorney present."

"Why is that?"

Ms. Navarro said nothing, so Lottie gave a very educated guess. "Because Mitch Kesslar and Ms. Navarro here were having an affair." After all, a man didn't share the keys of his Ferrari with just anyone.

Within the hour, Jessie Navarro's attorney arrived, and she gave her official statement. She and Mitch Kesslar had been having an on-and-off affair for the past five years that started when she'd been the marketing manager for K-2. Mitch had even given her the seed money to start her own company.

"Pretty generous of the guy to fund a competitor," Bradley said.

"He was funding a hard working employee and well-respected colleague." Ms. Navarro's eyes misted. "Mitch was generous to many."

But not to his son. Lottie really wanted to get her hands on that boy's voice mail records.

Last night, Navarro called Mitch after six and congratulated him on the Aspen deal. He told her to come on over and they would celebrate. She got busy with some loose ends at the office, and when she got to the K-2 offices, he was gone. She saw the Ferrari was still in the parking lot.

"His partner, Derrick Kemp, was always good about taking Mitch's keys when he drank too much," Navarro said.

Still wanting to hook up with Kesslar, Navarro drove to his house. "When I got there, Mitch was upset, complaining about his lazy son who wanted to live the high life but didn't want to work. I offered to get Mitch out of his bad mood, but he sent me packing. So I called a taxi that took me back to my car at the K-2 office."

"Did you go straight home?" Bradley asked.

"I stopped at King Soopers and bought two pints of ice cream."

"And for the rest of evening?"

"I ate ice cream and watched mindless reality TV."

"No one can vouch for your whereabouts at ten twenty-one?"

"Just Ben and Jerry."

Bradley hopped to his feet like an eager puppy. He was getting close. He had a suspect with means, motive, and opportunity. Hell, the woman's fingerprints were on the murder weapon. "You'll need to come down to the station with us," Bradley said.

The attorney raised a hand, but Navarro waved him off. "Before you even think about arresting me, Detective Bradley, you need to see the threats." She reached

into a desk drawer and pulled out a stack of letters and
envelopes.

"Threats?" Bradley asked.

"Five year's worth. All from Melanie Kesslar warning
me to stay away from her husband. In one she threatened
to kill me *and* Mitch."

***

"You're thinking again," Lottie said as they drove to
the Kesslar's mansion.

"Melanie Kesslar was in Denver at the time of the killing, so she couldn't have killed her husband, but that
doesn't mean she didn't pay someone to kill him. The
woman has piles of money. I need to check financials. See
if she's withdrawn any large sums."

When they reached the Kesslar mansion, Melanie
Kesslar met them at the front door where Bradley
showed her a company head shot of Jessie Navarro, her
red lips glistening on the glossy paper. "Do you recognize
this woman?"

Melanie Kesslar glanced at the photo for a half second.
"That would be my husband's mistress." She fanned
away the photo as if fanning stink off rotten apples. "Yes,
I know about her along with the others."

"The others?" Bradley asked.

"Let's see, there's Helene, the secretary, and Maddie,
one of Andrew's college girlfriends. Plus, there was that
girl from the country club with the red Miata. I think her
name was Tabby." Melanie Kesslar pushed the hair back
from her tear-stained face. "I knew Mitch like I knew

myself. He loved good food, great champagne, shiny toys, and women. The more the merrier. He was a man of excess. He didn't know when to say when."

No kidding. Too much to drink left him incapacitated. Had one of his many women, present company included, left him dead with a single blow?

"And these other women didn't bother you?" Bradley continued.

"Of course they did. I begged Mitch to stop seeing them, even threatened to leave."

"You sent threatening letters to Jessie Navarro. Pretty clear messages, especially the one, *Leave my husband alone or you both die.*"

"That...that...was just words." Mrs. Kessler flicked her hands with a dismissive shrug. "It was a way to blow off steam, but it worked. The woman finally backed off, which was good because Mitch wasn't capable of self-control."

"But you stayed with him?" Bradley motioned to the entryway filled with gilded tables and fancy flower arrangements. "Because you didn't want to give up this?"

"Because I loved him, Detective Bradley. *Him.*" She fisted her hand and laid it against the center of her chest. "Mitch had my heart long before he had the millions, and even if the millions all went away, he'd still have me. He was kind and generous, and above all, loving. I can't imagine life without him." The woman's voice cracked.

A taxi pulled into the drive and Lottie nodded to both Bradley and Mrs. Kesslar. "That's for me. I'll be going now."

She was halfway down the drive when Bradley

grabbed her arm. "Where are you going?"

"To my retirement party."

"You can't leave now."

She tapped at her watch. "It's five o'clock. Time to clock out."

He pointed at the open door where Melanie Kesslar stood. "We're not done interviewing the woman who made a death threat against our victim."

"I am." Lottie put her hand on the young detective's arm. "Because unlike Mitch Kesslar, I know when to say when." For more than three decades she lived and loved her job, but it was time to stop. There were young, smart, hardworking pups, like Bradley here, to carry on the good work. "I have absolute faith that you, Detective Bradley, will find Mitch Kesslar's killer, and justice will be served."

"The first forty-eight hours are crucial."

"Then stop your yakking and get back to work." She climbed into the taxi. "And when you get a break, come down to the station for the party. There's gonna be a chocolate fountain."

Chapter Four

The gray-haired receptionist who'd worked the front desk for the past two decades looked up and frowned. "Sergeant King, what are you doing here?"

"I'm done for the day."

"Already?"

Lottie lifted a peep-toe. "My feet are tired."

"Really?" The receptionist was still frowning. "Do you need to sit down, or can I get you something?"

Lottie couldn't help but smile. She knew what was going on. The receptionist was stalling for time. Her co-workers were probably still setting up. Balloons, streamers, maybe even a table with a present or two. Old Enrique got a money tree at his retirement party. If she got one, she'd take all the green bills and take a Caribbean cruise. She and her old friend, Ruthie, who was murdered last month in a case that had knocked the wind out of Lottie's sails, always talked about cruising after they retired. Yep, she'd take a cruise and toast Ruthie as she stood on the deck with the wind in her hair and salty sea spray on her face.

Lottie took her time as she walked through the station. This place had been her second home, these men and women her second family. She dabbed at the corner of her eyes. Damn dust this time of year.

In the hallway she spotted Doyle, the custodian, carrying a ladder out of the conference room. Yep, definitely balloons. Maybe even a piñata because—hot damn—there'd be kids: her grands, Traynor's twins, maybe even Bradley's baby.

"Hey there, Doyle." Lottie winked at the custodian. "Keeping busy?"

"Yep. Got the windows washed, rugs cleaned, and a few lights replaced."

She settled her hand on the conference room door. It was so quiet in there she could hear the canned air moving through the vents. She sniffed. Was that chocolate?

She opened the door and flipped on the light.

Not a drop of chocolate in sight.

She balled her hands on hips. The entire place was empty. Come to think of it, the parking garage was empty, too. Granted, most of her colleagues were dealing with the hostage situation, but that didn't mean there weren't any party plans. She tapped a shiny red shoe. So the party must not be at the station. Maybe they needed something bigger and more festive, something where folks could bring their families, because she was sure her family would be there.

Her house was tiny, but she had a great backyard. Big ol' fire pit. Thick branches on the peach tree that would look pretty all lit up with them twinkle lights. And a wide porch with an electrical outlet for the chocolate fountain.

***

Lottie pulled into her driveway and gave kudos to whoever was in charge of her *surprise* retirement party. He or she was doing one hell of a job. On the drive through her neighborhood she spotted no familiar cars. Even her daughter Tiarra's driveway was empty, the lights in the house off. Someone was working hard to pull the wool over her eyes because they knew she was a good detective.

As Lottie climbed the porch steps, she debated what kind of face to wear. The folks inside would expect a surprise face, especially the grands. Wide eyes. Open mouth. Maybe even a shaky hand to her heart. Yep, that would tickle the kids.

She jiggled her keys extra loud, giving everyone time to get ready.

She walked in the door, shock-face in place.

"What the hell?" she called out to no one because *no one* was in the room. Her peep-toes clacking, she checked the backyard. Equally empty.

She turned in a circle under the old peach tree. Where were her people? Where was her big send-off? She dug her phone out of her purse and dialed Tiarra. "Where are you, young lady?"

"At the school," her daughter said. "It's curriculum night."

"What about my surprise party?"

"Surprise party?"

"For my retirement." Frustration threatened to pop a few curls from the knot of hair on the back of her head.

Tiarra laughed. "Like you're going to retire."

"I did. Today."

"Ha-ha, Ma. You can tell me another joke when I get home. Right now I need to go meet with Emmie's math teacher. Em's having a hard time with fractions. Then I need to meet with the president of the PTO about the multi-cultural festival. Will's juggling the triplets. Ma, are you there?"

Lottie leaned against the trunk of the old tree. "I really did it, Tee. No more late nights. No more chasing Big Bads. No more shiny badge." Lottie slid to the soft earth with a plunk. "I'm no longer a detective with the Colorado Springs Police Department."

A fast breath of air rushed over the other end of the line. "You're serious."

"As a heartbeat."

Short pause. Big cheer. "This is great, Ma. Amazing. But unexpected. We didn't think you'd really do it or we would have done something. I mean we..."

"It's okay, Tee. Get to class and get things worked out with Emmie's math teacher. She needs to know fractions when she becomes the managing director of the International Monetary Fund. We'll celebrate tomorrow."

"No!" Giddy laughter sashayed across the phone line. "Tonight. After we're done, Will can pick up some ice cream and a cake."

"Avoid the Mountain Point Bank off Boulder. Hostage situation. Roads closed." And where every available man and woman from the station was. A wave—so tiny it was really only a ripple—of envy washed over her, not because she wasn't working to preserve life but because she was alone.

She pressed her palm against the old peach tree, its limbs as brown and weathered and wrinkled as hers.

"Ahh, Ma, you okay?"

Lottie hopped to her feet. No need to get all gloom and doomy tonight. "I'm good." Yep, she was alive and had her health, a few pennies in the bank, and plenty of family and friends. Eventually they'd celebrate her retirement. Until then, she wasn't going to let a lack of party hold her back. Even though she was in unchartered waters, she was ready for a whole new journey. "Now get off the phone and go talk to those school people. Love you."

Inside the house, Lottie plugged her cell phone into the charger. Her fingers hovered above the keypad. Nope, she wasn't going to do it. She wasn't going to call Traynor to get the low-down on the hostage situation. Nor was she going to check in on Junior about the Kesslar murder. She was done, and later tonight she'd celebrate with the ones who mattered most, her girls and the grands. Of course, Chantelle, her oldest daughter, wouldn't be there because she was still in South America doctoring folks. Lottie had raised a doctor, a nutritionist, and a librarian. Not bad for a life's work, and she wasn't done living yet.

The phone rang. She jumped at it.

"Listen, Ma, we ran into a little issue," Tiarra said. "Will got called into a shift at the hospital, and I have to finish up curriculum night on my own. I'm sorry, but can we postpone the party?"

"No worries, baby-girl. Life happens. Give my sweeties a hug, and we'll party tomorrow."

No party tonight.

The thought slammed her more than she wanted to admit. Because, damn it, she wanted a party, and if no one had time to throw one for her, she'd make her own.

***

Lottie pulled up to Monroe's, a cop bar a few blocks from the station. Tonight none of her colleagues sat on the barstools. They were all still attending to business.

"Hey, Sarge." Donny, the bartender, set a napkin in front of her. "You want the regular?"

Which would be a Tom Collins, two maraschino cherries. "Nope. Tonight I'm celebrating." Today hadn't gone exactly as planned, but stuff in her life rarely did. That was okay. She knew how to ride out stormy seas. "What should I have?"

"Champagne," Donny suggested.

She pictured Mitch Kesslar who'd downed one too many glasses of bubbly, but unlike him, she knew when to say when. "Sure."

Donny puttered around the bar and, *Pop!*

Lottie ducked. Then laughed when she realized the sound was not a gunshot but a champagne cork. You could take the badge off the girl, but it left a mighty big imprint.

She sipped the champagne, the bubbles tickling her nose. On the television at the far end of the bar, a news reporter was giving an update on the hostage situation. She got up and switched the channel. Tonight she didn't want to be reminded of that nasty one percent.

Sometime during glass number two, the bell on the door clanged, and hair the color and texture of a haystack made its way in. Sure enough, Scott Traynor's nose was as red as her shoes.

"That nose is going to blister," she said when he plopped onto the barstool next to her with a weary sigh.

"I know. I need to get my own screen."

"I left a tube on your desk." She motioned to Donny to serve her former partner a glass of bubbly. "How did it go?"

"We just collared the final gunmen. No shots fired. No loss of life."

She clinked her glass against his. "I wouldn't expect anything less."

Again the bell jangled, and three of the boys from homicide walked in, all looking beat but smiling. At her. A few minutes later, the lieutenant and his wife arrived. One by one the members of her CSPD family trickled into the bar. Drinks flowed, and at some point, a delivery kid walked in with a tower of pizzas.

Lottie worked the room, her feet no longer tired. A good hour into the world's best retirement party, Bradley arrived, but unlike everyone else, he wasn't smiling.

She elbowed her way through the crowd to Bradley who was diving into a pizza box. Poor kid must have worked his way through the dinner hour.

"Happy retirement, Sarge," he said around a mouthful of mushrooms and sausage.

After he inhaled two slices, she asked. "So where are you on the Kesslar case?"

"Checked Melanie Kesslar's financials and found no

large sums of money taken from any accounts. No un-known calls on her cell phone record. Right now I can't find any link to any hired guns."

"What about the mistress/competitor/tequila con-noisseur?"

"I learned Jessie Navarro has some serious money problems and even found an e-mail begging Kesslar to let her in on the Aspen deal, which as we both know didn't happen."

"That's the kind of stuff that gets a gal a little hot un-der the collar."

Bradley nodded. "I visited Navarro's condo complex, which has a pretty slick video security system, but there's no record of Navarro or her car leaving the premises last night."

Lottie was hoping this kid would get a quick collar. There was nothing like a big fat check in the win column to take the green off the greenhorn. "What about the coroner's report?"

Bradley held up his iPad. "Just got a copy. It'll be my bedtime reading."

"For the record, that's a mighty fast turnaround. The folks at the coroner's office are partial to apple pie. You might want to take them a few." She held out her hand. "Let's see that report."

"Here? Now?" He flattened his iPad against his chest. "It's your retirement party."

"Exactly. It's *my* party, and I'll do what I want to." She pried the iPad from his fingers.

They found a quiet booth in the back where Bradley called up the coroner's report on his iPad. Blood tox showed Kesslar's BAC was .25. A few more sips of Señor Patron and he would have pickled his brain. She scrolled to the next page and studied the drawing of the attacker striking Mitch Kesslar with the bottle. Interesting.

"What do you make of this?" Lottie asked, tapping her finger against the drawing where the attacker and Kesslar stood face-to-face.

"Kesslar got a good look at his killer and saw him lift the bottle. Since there are no defense wounds, I'm guessing Kesslar knew the attacker and had no reason to suspect the bottle would end up colliding with his skull."

"And?" Lottie prompted. There was a party going on, and she didn't have time for this youngster to puzzle through the drawing. She pointed to the contusion on Kesslar's temple.

"He was hit on the right side of the head."

"Exactly. By an assailant facing him, and that means..." She circled the air with her hand.

"That our killer was most likely left-handed."

"Give the student an A-plus." She grabbed her bag from the back of the barstool. "You ready to go?"

"Where?"

"To visit the only left-handed suspect we talked to."

"You know that?"

"Yep." She nudged him toward the door. "You do too."

He sunk in his heels. "I do?"

"Of course you do. Picture the neighbor dialing up information on his cell phone, the wife pouring tea, the son swinging the golf club, the partner unfastening his scooter helmet, the mistress handing you those letters."

Bradley worked his jaw. Despite the party shouts and laughter, she could hear the grinding of bone and teeth. Then he smiled.

***

Derrick Kemp lived in a two-bedroom townhouse exactly one mile from the Kesslar mansion. He answered the door in a baggy pair of sweats and old Nike T-shirt. "Is there something I can do for you, detectives?"

"You can tell us why," Bradley said.

Kemp took off his glasses and rubbed the bridge of his nose. "I'm sorry?"

"Why did you kill Mitch Kesslar?" Bradley asked.

The boy was blunt. Good. They had a party to get to.

Kemp slipped his glasses in his shirt pocket. "What are you talking about? I had an alibi. My poker buddies can verify we were playing that night."

"Online buddies. You were playing poker online."

"It's legal."

"You're a numbers guy, right? So let's take a look at the numbers," Bradley said. "You live one mile from Kesslar. At ten at night, the traffic is light. Even if you hit one or two traffic lights, you can make it there in about three minutes, four tops. The front door isn't locked, so you waltz inside and find Kesslar on the back porch. Another minute. Maybe you tell him you wanted to make sure he got home okay. Or maybe you argue. I'm not sure. What I do know is that you picked up the bottle of tequila and hit him. Two more minutes."

Kemp crossed his arms over his chest. "You have my

prints on the bottle as proof?"

"No, you were wearing gloves because you wear gloves, a helmet, and leather jacket when you ride. Which gets us back to numbers. You hit Kesslar, and he falls into the pond. His blood alcohol content is .25, which puts him in a near stupor. He struggles in the water but can't get out. Another two minutes pass, maybe three, and he's gone. Then it's another four minutes and you're back home. That makes fourteen minutes. Is my math right, Sergeant King?"

Lottie nodded. "You sure do know how to add, Detective Bradley."

"I was playing poker online," Kemp insisted.

"Except for the bathroom and beer break everyone took from 10:15 to 10:30."

Kemp ran his hands through his hair, the rumpled professor look giving way to a scared-as-hell murder suspect.

Bradley kept swinging. "The numbers add up, Mr. Kemp."

Kemp's eyes shifted left then right.

"Don't think about running. It's two against one." Bradley's voice was soft but hard as steel.

Kemp's shoulders slumped. The guy wasn't even going to fight. Makes for a kind of boring final case, but she'd take the W.

"Numbers," Kemp said.

Bradley reached for the handcuffs at his waist. "Numbers?"

"You asked why I did it. It's a matter of numbers. I lost more than I earned. Gambling. The guy I borrowed from was threatening to zero me out if I didn't pay."

It was starting to add up.

"You had a life insurance policy out on your partner," Lottie said.

"Enough to bail me out of trouble."

***

Bradley and Lottie watched the cruiser drive away with Kemp in the backseat.

"Another soul who didn't know when to say when," Lottie said. "He and Kesslar were fifty-fifty partners. Imagine the money he must have lost with his gambling addiction."

"Some people don't have the willpower to stop." Bradley nudged her arm. "Just like you, Sarge. Here it is your retirement party, and you're still working."

"Nope. I didn't do a lick of work tonight." She poked him in the rib. "It was all you, Detective Bradley. Congratulations. You'll never fill these shoes," she waggled a red peep-toe at him, "but you're going to make a fine homicide investigator."

"You're serious? You're done."

"I had the bon-voyage party, and my ship's about to sail."

Bradley reached into the pocket of his blazer. "Then I guess it's time to give you this." He handed her a bar of limp chocolate. "It's been in my pocket all afternoon. Sorry it got a little melted."

Lottie took the melted chocolate bar. Not a chocolate fountain, but close.

Peach Margarita

Heavenly when made with fresh white peaches at the peak of summer!

Yield: Serves 1; Prep time: 5 minutes; Total time: 5 minutes

Ingredients
1/2 cup peach puree (about two medium peaches, skin removed)
1.5 ounces silver tequila
.75 ounces triple sec
1 tablespoon simple syrup
1 lime, juiced
Ice
Sea salt
Lime and peach slice (optional)

Directions
1. Combine peach puree, tequila, triple sec, simple syrup and lime.
2. Wet rim of serving glass. Dip in sea salt.
3. Pour peach mixture and ice into prepped glass and garnish, if desired.

Author's Note: My Guy is a big margarita fan, and living a few hours from Mexico, we've encountered some great tequilas in local restaurants and during our trips to nearby Puerto Peñasco. The Gran Patron Platinum that's used as the murder weapon in Smooth Sailing is one of the best, especially if you like your tequila on the rocks. If I were at Lottie's retirement party, I would buy her one of these. Enjoy!

From the creative kitchen of award-winning author
Shelley Coriell
www.shelleycoriell.com

Message from Shelley Coriell

I'm thrilled and honored that you read ROUGH DAY and spent time with my salty and sassy Detective Lottie King! If you enjoyed this collection of short stories:

- Please check out the complete Detective Lottie King Mystery Short Stories Series
    Rough Day, Vol. 1
    New Shoes , Vol. 2
    Thin Ice , Vol. 3
    Tangled Truths, Vol. 4
    Broken Heart , Vol. 5
    Dark Secret, Vol. 6

- Sign up for my non-spammy newsletter at http://www.shelleycoriell.com/newsletter and receive information about new releases.

- Write a review and post to Amazon or your favorite bookish e-tailer. Reviews are crucial to authors like me in reaching other readers.

- Follow me on twitter @ShelleyCoriell or like my Facebook page at http://facebook.com/ShelleyCoriellAuthor.

If you'd like to read an excerpt from *THE BROKEN*— my award-winning, full-length romantic thriller where Detective Lottie King first walks onto the page in a pair of splashy high heels—please turn the page.

Excerpt from

The Broken

Apostles Series #1

Available from Grand Central Forever

Journalist Kate Johnson is on the run, hiding from a serial killer who needs her dead and a past that left her scarred. Legendary FBI profiler Hayden Reed is on the hunt, desperate to track down Kate and gain her trust, for it's her darkest secret that can stop a madman who leaves in his wake broken mirrors and broken lives.

Chapter One

Tuesday, June 9, 1:48 A.M.
Mancos, Colorado

The cry was low and tortured, pulled from the gut of a man who'd been to hell and back.

Kate Johnson threw off her covers and grabbed the box of paperclips she kept on her nightstand. "I'm coming, Smokey Joe," she called even though the old man couldn't hear her. He was too far away, trapped in a time and place known only to his tormented mind. She tore down the steps of the cabin and into Smokey's bedroom.

"Safety pins! Where the hell are my safety pins?" Smokey's hands clawed at the covers she'd tucked around him four hours ago. "Dammit to hell! I need those pins."

Kate took one of his hands in hers and dropped a handful of paperclips onto his palm. "Here you go."

His knobby fingers clamped around the bits of metal, and he dipped them in a frantic but practiced rhythm. Eventually his cries died off and gave way to moans. Then came the sobs. They were the worst.

As she had dozens of times over the past six months, she sank to her knees beside his bed and gathered him in her arms. Papery skin over old bones. The sour-sweet smell of cold sweat. Her cheek rubbed against the sprigs of gray hair on his head. As the sobs tapered off and his trembling ceased, she looked at her arms and shook her head. How could a hug, nothing more than two arms, *her arms*, stop a war?

When the old man's breathing returned to normal, he opened his sightless eyes. "That you, Katy-lady?"

She squeezed his bony knee. "Yes."

Relief smoothed the lines of terror twisting his face.

She left his bedside and opened the top drawer of the bureau. "Who was it?"

He inched himself to an upright position. "Never got a name on this one. He wasn't talking by the time ground grunts got him in the chopper. Mortar round blew off half his neck."

"What do you remember about him?" This was another thing she didn't understand, Smokey's need to relive the pains of the past. Yesterday's horrors should be bundled up and tucked away. They had no place in this world. She reached into the drawer for a clean nightshirt.

"He had red hair, color of a firecracker, and he held a picture of his momma in his hand. We lost him before we got to DaNang, but I made sure the hospital crew got the picture and told them to tell that boy's momma she'd been right there with her son when he needed her, offering comfort only a momma can."

Mommas don't offer comfort. The thought snuck up on her, a jarring uppercut to the chin.

"Katy-lady, you okay?"

The bureau drawer slammed shut. "I'm fine."

She handed Smokey Joe the clean nightshirt and sat on the foot of the bed. That's when she noticed the soft voices coming from the radio on the nightstand. A late-night talk show host was talking to William from Michigan about a school shooting in New Jersey that left two eleven year olds dead. "This!" She jabbed a hand at the radio. "What is *this*?"

"Don't know." Smokey raised his gaze to the ceiling. "Can't see."

She snapped off the radio, silencing the voices. "You were listening to the news before bed again, weren't you?"

"You going to start nagging me? I don't pay you to ride my ass."

"No, you pay me to take care of you, and if you don't want to take out any new help-wanted ads, listen to me. Your doctor said no news before bedtime. Those stories from the Mid East bring back too many war memories." And trigger nightmares of a time when he desperately tried to save bloody and broken bodies with only a handful of safety pins and a heart full of hope.

His gnarled fingers fumbled with the buttons of his sweat-soaked nightshirt. She reached over to help.

"I wasn't listening to no war news. There was another one of them Barbie murders. This one right here in Colorado. All the stations are yammering about it."

Barbie murders? What an insane world, filled with criminals without conscience, a public fascinated by the gory and gruesome, and media ready to unite the two for the sake of ratings. She didn't miss the crazy world of broadcast news and had no regrets that she hadn't seen a newscast in almost three years, not since she'd *been* the news.

She unfastened Smokey's next two buttons. "So a *Barbie* was killed?"

"Yep. Course the coppers don't call 'em Barbies. That's just my name, but I think that makes six now, all TV gals, all stabbed to death in their homes."

She grew still. "Broadcast journalists? Stabbed?"

"Yeah, not too pretty, either. Each gal had more than fifty knife wounds. Now why the hell does someone need to stab a body fifty times?"

Her hand sought the raised, jagged line below her right eye. *Because twenty-five isn't enough to kill?*

"I'll tell you why." Smokey jabbed a crooked index finger at his temple. "He ain't right in the head."

Kate slipped the shirt off Smokey's bony shoulders, her own shoulders relaxing. As an investigative reporter she'd seen up close the machinations of the criminal mind. She knew the mean and twisted and evil that perpetuated crimes against humanity. There were plenty of bad people in this world, plenty of knife-wielding crazies, and the twenty-five scars that criss-crossed her body had nothing to do with Smokey's *Barbies*. "Haven't we both determined the world in general isn't right in the head?"

"But this guy's sick, scary sick. He does that creepy thing with the mirrors."

The curtains on Smokey's window shifted with the night breeze, and the hairs on the back of her neck stood on end. "Mirrors?"

"After he kills them Barbies, the screwball goes around breaking every mirror in the house. He shatters every single one. You ever heard of such a crazy thing?"

Sounds ricocheted through her head. The swoosh of a hammer. The crack of glass. The obscenely happy tinkle of falling mirror fragments.

Smokey's shirt, soaked in sweat and terror, fell from her hand.

Yes, Smokey, I heard it. I saw it. I lived it.

***

Tuesday, June 9, 4 A.M.
Colorado Springs, Colorado

Hayden Reed stared at the shards of mirror that once covered an entire wall in Shayna Thomas's entryway. The largest piece was no bigger than two inches square.

Insanity was one hell of a wrecking ball.

He squatted to study the destruction, looking for trace—blood, footprints, hairs, fibers, anything that would lead him to the killer he'd been tracking for five months. All he saw in the broken mirror were distorted bits of his face, a macabre reflection of a man who'd been slammed by a wrecking ball of his own.

Hayden stood, and Parker Lord's voice echoed through his head. "Hold off on the Colorado slaying," his boss had said. "Hatch can cover for you and bring you up to speed when you get things wrapped up in Tucson with your family."

His family was fine.

Time to hunt for a butcher. But first he needed to track down Sergeant Lottie King.

A uniform directed Hayden through the living room and down a hallway where he came face to face with a short, round African-American woman. Her crinkly gray hair hugged her head in a tight knot, and she wore a simple navy suit and a Glock 22 holstered under her left arm. On her feet were the highest, reddest heels he'd ever seen outside a whorehouse.

"Chief warned me some FBI hotshot was coming in, and you got hotshot written all over you." The sergeant crossed her arms over her chest. "My boys said you're one of Parker Lord's men, a fucking apostle. That true?"

Hayden noticed the change in her tone. It happened often at the mention of Parker's Special Criminal Investigative Unit, a small group of FBI specialists known for working outside the box and, according to some, outside the law. Some media pundit nicknamed them the Apostles. Like Parker, Hayden didn't care about names, only justice. "Yes."

"Heard you boys play by a different set of rules."

He clasped his hands behind his back. "We don't play."

Her jaw squared in a challenge as she jutted her chin toward the shattered mirror in the hallway. "So tell me, Agent I-Don't-Play, what's your take?"

Shayna Thomas had been found dead in her bedroom six hours ago. Multiple stab wounds. No signs of sexual trauma. Shattered mirrors. All the earmarks of another Broadcaster Butcher slaying. Hayden pointed to a spot three feet down the hall. "The unsub stood there. One strike. Used a long-handled, blunt instrument he brought with him. Carefully positioned his body out of the glass trajectory. You'll find no blood near this or any of the other broken mirrors. You'll also find no footprints, no fingerprints, no trace, and no witnesses." The other Butcher crime scenes had been freakishly void of evidence.

The sergeant locked him in a stare down. He studied the wide, steady stance of those high heels, the indignant puff of her chest, and the single corkscrew of hair that stuck out above her right ear.

"And your take, Sergeant King?"

The police sergeant's nostrils flared. "I think we got us one fucked-up son of a bitch, and I can't wait to nail his ass to the splintered seat of a cold, dark cell where he'll never see the light of day."

Early in his law enforcement career, he'd learned there were two kinds of people behind the shield: those seeking personal gain—a paycheck, ego strokes, power— and those seeking justice. Like him, the woman in the red shoes was one of the latter. Hayden unclasped his hands. "And I can't wait to hand you a hammer."

A smile wrinkled the corner of her eyes, and he saw what he needed: respect.

"Damn glad you're here, Agent Reed."

"For the record, Sergeant King, I hear you aren't much of a slouch, either."

"Ahh, a pretty face *and* a smooth talker. I think I might be able to work with you." The smile in her eyes dimmed as she motioned him to follow her down the hall.

"Timeline?" Hayden asked.

"A man out walking his dog hears breaking glass as

he passes Thomas's house. He calls the station at 10:32. Beat officer arrives at 10:37. He makes repeated shout outs, but no one responds. He looks through the front window, sees the broken mirror, and calls for back up. When the second uniform arrives, they enter and discover the victim in the master bedroom."

"Positive ID?"

"Confirmed. Shayna Thomas. Homeowner."

"Current status?"

"Crime Scene Division's still processing." Sergeant King's red shoes drew to a halt. "This is one mother of a scene."

"Blood." Hayden didn't frame the single word as a question. They'd found excessive amounts of blood at the other Butcher crime scenes, five since January.

"It's the fucking Red Sea in there. You better watch those shiny shoes of yours." Lottie pointed to the door in front of them. "I'm warning you. It ain't pretty."

Wrongful death never was.

Inside the bedroom, blood peppered four walls, striped the white down comforter, and clung to the fan centered on the ceiling. The victim lay on the ground in front of a dresser. Blood soaked her T-shirt and jogging shorts and matted her hair. She was a brunette, slim, probably attractive. Hard to tell. Lacerations decussated her face, arms, neck, and abdomen, but as he expected, the V at her legs was blood and injury-free.

He saved the hands for last. He always did. It was hard to think clearly after seeing them, hard to stop being the dispassionate evaluator. Drawing air into his tightening lungs, he turned to Shayna Thomas's bloody hands.

They rested on her breasts, fingers intertwined as if in prayer, a gesture of peace amidst the chaos of murder.

For a moment he lowered his eyelids and calmed the rage that simmered in a place he refused to acknowledge.

Those bloody hands beckoned him, pulled him in, and wouldn't let go. His boss, Parker Lord, was wrong. Hayden needed to be here.

***

Tuesday, June 9, 4:03 A.M.
Mancos, Colorado

Run. Fast and far.

Kate's hands shook worse than Smokey Joe's as she yanked the saddlebags out of the closet and slammed them on her bed. From the bureau, she hauled out the few things she called her own: underwear, scarves, T-shirts, chambray over shirts, jeans, and her leathers. She jammed all but the leathers into the bags and threw in her brown contacts and hair dye. Meager belongings compared to her on-air days, a time when she wore a different face. A face hacked by a madman. A madman who hadn't stopped after the butcher job on her.

The wooden floor creaked behind her. She dropped her leathers and spun. Something shifted in the shadow of the doorway. She reached for the ceramic lamp on the nightstand then set it down when Smokey stepped out of the darkness.

He cleared his throat with a rough cough. "Are you

taking off?"

Her hand dropped to her side, and she tried not to look into his sightless eyes, eyes filled with confusion and something else. *Oh God, please don't let him look at me like that.* "Yes." What more could she say? *I'm sorry for disappointing you. I'm sorry for leaving because there's a madman roaming the country who vowed to kill me and who has since murdered six other women.*

She yanked the saddlebag zippers closed. How stupid to think she could stop running, stupid to stay in one place so long, and stupid to put an old, blind man like Smokey Joe in danger. She picked up the leather pants and jammed her legs into them. The Shayna Thomas attack had occurred in Colorado Springs, only three-hundred miles from Smokey Joe's cabin in Southwestern Colorado.

Smokey scratched the stubble on his chin. "That big order? You got it done?"

"Order?" She grabbed her helmet from the top shelf of the closet.

"That gal out of San Diego who wants all them angels. You get 'em done?"

Kate couldn't think about their online jewelry store or tourmaline angels. She thought only about getting away. "Order's done. It's boxed and on the table."

"I'll ship it." One of Smokey's slippers, the color and texture of beef jerky, whisked across the floor. "Where should I send your cut?"

"You keep it." She needed no connections to Smokey Joe, no trail that could put him in the sights of a knife-wielding madman.

Smokey nodded and shuffled away. The sound of his ratty slippers on the floor she polished weekly pounded in her head and tugged at her heart.

The past six months with Smokey Joe had been peaceful, and after being on the run for more than two years, she'd needed the rest and recharge. During her time here in the scrub canyons and pine forests of Southwestern Colorado, she hadn't thought about the past or the future. She'd been simply living, living simply.

She flung her saddlebags over her shoulder—amazing how little a person needed to live—and rushed down the steps to the bottom floor. She bolted through the kitchen but ground to a halt at the backdoor.

Turning quickly, she set the timer for Smokey's morning coffee, flicked on the bread machine, and left an urgent voice message with his case manager. Only then did she slip out of the house, deadbolt the lock, and escape into the safe cover of darkness.

To read more, check out **The Broken** (http://www.shelleycoriell.com/the-broken).

Acknowledgement

A world of thanks to all the good people who've been in my corner as I jumped off yet another cliff in order to tell the stories of my heart: Jessica Faust, my fierce and wise agent; Sydney Strand, my bold and blunt critique partner; Colorado Springs PD, especially Homicide Detective Debbie Adelbush (Ret.); Colorado friends Arjay and Eva Rhoads and Donnell Ann Bell; copy editor Linda Style; and cover designer Clarissa Yeo.

Finally, to my sister, Paula Slone, who has been and always will be my best friend and biggest cheerleader. Paula, you may not swear as much as Lottie, but you have her rock-solid strength, fiery passion, and big ol' heart. Thanks for believing in me!

Marnie McCann

SHELLEY CORIELL is an award-winning author of mysteries, romantic thrillers, and novels for teens. Her debut thriller was named one of *Publishers Weekly's* Best Books of the Year, and her other novels have been nominated for an RT Reviewers' Choice Award, Best Paperback Original of the Year from the International Thriller Writers, and a Kirkus Recommended Read. A former magazine editor and restaurant reviewer, Shelley lives in Arizona with her family and the world's neediest rescue weimaraner. You can find her at www.shelleycoriell.com and Twittering @ShelleyCoriell.

Made in the
USA
Middletown, DE